I0533604

# Such a Time as This

Rebecca Velez

*Such a Time as This*

Published in the U.S. by Rebecca Velez Books
Manchester, NH

Copyright © 2007 by Rebecca Velez. All rights reserved.
Second edition, 2018.

Scripture portions are taken from a combination of versions:
*The Holy Bible*, King James Version.
*The New International Version*®. NIV®.Copyright © 1973, 1978, 1984
by International Bible Society. Used by permission of Zondervan. All
rights reserved.
*The New American Standard Bible*®, copyright © 1960, 1962, 1963,
1968, 1971, 1972, 1973, 1975, 1977, 1995 by The Lockman
Foundation. Used by permission.

ISBN: 978-1-7322921-0-9
Library of Congress Control Number: 2018905540

*Such a Time as This* is a work of fiction. Names, characters, places,
and incidents either are the product of the author's imagination or
are used fictitiously. Any resemblance to actual events (other than
historical connections), locales, organizations, or persons, living or
dead, is entirely coincidental and beyond the intent of the author.

To my mom, who
shared her love of
reading with me

# Acknowledgments

Thanks to:

My mother-in-law, Madeline Butler, who helped me find Persian names;

Ken Meyers who advised me on Hebrew words;

My mother, Sharon Spires, who read several drafts, made suggestions for revisions, and encouraged me to finish;

Ramona Tucker and Jeff Nesbit of Capstone Fiction, who helped me realize a long-time goal by first publishing this book.

"Who knows but
that you have come
to royal position for

*such a time as this*?"

Esther 4:14

# Cast of Characters

Adin—Rachel's twin daughter
Amaris—a Jewess who becomes friends with Rachel
Anezka—a concubines from the Caucasus; Esther's friend
Artasyras—owner of a metal shop
**Artaxerxes** (Arty)—Isis and Xerxes' son adopted by Esther
Artystone—wife of Otanes
Atossa—a maid

**Bigthan**—chamberlain who plotted to assassinate Xerxes

**Carshena**—one of Xerxes' counselors

David—the Jew whom Esther planned to marry; leader of the
Jewish forces against Haman
Della—a concubine from Sipylus; Esther's friend
Dinah—a Jewish midwife

**Ezra**—a Jew

Hadassah—Esther's Jewish name; Esther's namesake, Ezra and
Rachel's eldest daughter
**Haman**—the king's favored counselor
**Hatach**—a chamberlain in the palace
**Hegai**—keeper of the virgins at the Persian palace
Herah—the wife of Memucan

Isis—a concubine from Egypt who became Esther's chief rival
Joel—Rachel's twin son

**Memucan**—one of the seven princes of Persia and the king's counselor

Mima—the head concubine when Esther arrived at the palace

Mithridates—head of the Persian weavers

Mitra—a princess concubine

**Mordecai**—Esther's adoptive father; a palace doorman

Nasha—mother of Artystone; chief midwife to Xerxes' harem

Oibares—Haman's brother-in-law

Otanes—a Persian soldier who befriends Esther

Parmys—one of Esther's maids

**Parshandatha** (Parsha)—Haman's eldest son

Rachel—Esther's dearest Jewish friend

Rebekah—Rachel's daughter

Sarah—Esther's grandmother

Sasha—an Indian princess

Smerdis—palace chef

Sparamizes—Isis and Xerxes' oldest son, adopted by Esther

**Tarshish**—one of the seven princes of Persia

**Teresh**—a chamberlain

**Xerxes**—the Persian king

**Zeresh**—wife of Haman

# Glossary

Abba—Hebrew for father

Ahura-Mazda—Zoroastrian deity of good

Apadana—audience hall for the king and his subjects

Ahriman—Zoroastrian deity of evil

Bet 'amma—house of the people, later called a synagogue

Cubit—an ancient measurement of about 18 inches

Parasang—Persian measure of distance, about 3 miles

Qanat—irrigation pond

Shalom—literally peace, a greeting of hello or good-bye

Softa—Hebrew for grandmother

Yehud—Judah

# 1

# Caught in the Bazaar

She feared the soldiers would hear the thumping of her heart. They were certainly out in force today. She never would have left the safety of the house if *softa* had not needed the medicinal herbs. Mordecai, her adoptive father, had warned her to stay at home unless it was absolutely necessary to go out, especially to a public place like the bazaar.

Pretending to shop, she hid behind a display of Persian robes. When no soldiers were in sight, she darted across to the old man who gathered and sold roots and herbs. Rachel remained as a lookout near the robe merchant.

The old man gave her an almost toothless grin. He had always liked Esther, and had missed seeing her for these past weeks. "So why haven't you come to see me lately?" he inquired. "Is the widow Sarah feeling better?"

"No, sir. She's very poorly, which is why I've come today." Esther hesitated. "I haven't been out much since the king's contest was announced. Father doesn't want me to come to harm."

"Ahh, I see. Yes, you're a beautiful damsel. The soldiers might force you to go up to the palace too. They have their orders, though

I hear many virgins arrive at the palace gate every day because they want to live the royal life. Here are your grandmother's herbs. Hurry home, and may Ahura-Mazda protect you."

But Esther and Rachel were unable to reach the streets branching out at the end of the bazaar before they heard heavy steps behind them. Esther hoped her veil would hide her. Both she and Rachel walked faster without hurrying too much. They were almost to the labyrinth of streets that would be their salvation. Might she never have to go out again.

Just then a street urchin dashed toward Esther, clutching a handful of pomegranates.

An angry stall keeper behind him shouted, "Stop, you worthless thief!"

The youngster changed direction, bearing full tilt into Esther. The force threw them both to the ground and dislodged her veil and headdress. Attempting to adjust her head covering with one hand and grab the nearby bag of herbs with the other, she started to stand, but a strong hand grasped her arm and helped her rise. As she looked into the face of her rescuer, she froze. She was gazing into the eyes of a Persian soldier.

"Looks like you found a right pretty one there, Otanes." His companion leered. "Let's get a better look at her." He roughly pulled off her veil. He paused when Esther's luxuriant black waves cascaded to her waist, as if surprised by exactly how beautiful she was.

Esther guessed he hadn't expected the rest of her to complement her face. All her life she had been told the Creator had given her an exquisite face. It was perfectly proportioned, with arching black eyebrows and lashes framing startling green eyes. Mordecai could not remember any relatives who had green eyes, though he said her great- grandmother had brown eyes with tints of green. But Esther's eyes were truly green, like the jade the jeweler Benjamin worked in his shop.

2

"Well, well, well, why hasn't a beautiful girl like you arrived at the palace yet for a shot at the crown?" the one called Otanes rumbled in a comfortable bass voice.

Unaware of Esther's plight, Rachel had already reached the edge of the bazaar before she turned to ask Esther which way she wanted to go home. She froze when she realized Esther had been apprehended by soldiers.

"Wait, there were two of them! Where's your friend?" demanded the first guard, twisting her arm so she would face him.

Through tears of pain, Esther discerned an evil face pockmarked by disease and felt his vile breath on her cheek. But Otanes's kinder hand intervened again as he took her arm and moved between her and her tormenter. "Careful. The king doesn't like his merchandise damaged by the likes of us. Come on. Let's get her up to Hegal at the palace. I'm sure the other one's long gone anyway."

Otanes' fellow soldier grumbled but remained at their sides as Esther once again rearranged her veil.

*Please, God*, Esther begged, knowing the impulsiveness of her friend, *protect Rachel. Don't let any harm come to her.*

Inadvertently, she glanced at the jumble of alleys to assure herself Rachel had reached safety, but the other guard had been watching her closely for such a slip. He immediately dashed toward Rachel, who stood, mouth agape, watching the fate of her best friend. "You, girl, come here."

Rachel shifted on her feet. Esther was uncertain whether her friend would run or obey the brutish guard. Usually quiet and reserved, Esther yelled with all her being, "Rachel, run!" Rachel immediately sprang away from her pursuer and disappeared in the maze beyond the marketplace. Esther knew her fleet friend could easily escape, if only no one else joined in the pursuit. Perhaps she herself would be able to slip away from this guard in all the confusion.

But to her dismay, Otanes tightened his grip. The wait seemed interminable to Esther, who alternately prayed for Rachel's deliverance and berated herself for giving her away. Eventually the other guard returned in a foul mood and without Rachel.

As Otanes guided them toward Shushan, Esther's thoughts turned to the palace. The rumors about palace life often tended to the bawdy—not that she'd heard much. Mordecai was one of the doormen at the palace gate, but he wasn't one to repeat gossip. Nonetheless, everyone had heard about King Xerxes stripping Queen Vashti of the crown. Softa Sarah had said the king deposed her because she refused to appear in the men's court at a drunken party. That would have been no place for a lady, her grandmother had added.

No one seemed quite sure what had happened to Vashti. Some said she was incarcerated in one of the stone towers. Others whispered she had been executed while a few swore she had been sent back to her family in Chaldea, completely disgraced. No worthy man would ever want to marry her, and she would never have children. Esther shuddered. What a horrible fate! The queen had been only twenty-two. Esther hoped she had been returned to her homeland since that had to be better than being kept here in disgrace, and perhaps discomfort.

Esther recalled other rumors she'd heard in the bazaar. Reportedly, the women of the harem fought tooth and nail as they competed for the king's favors for themselves and their children. So far the king had not named an heir, and according to the gossip, his eldest son had died of poisoning. Esther shuddered again. This wasn't the life she and Father had envisioned for her.

Otanes noticed Esther's shudders and squeezed her arm in a friendly way. "We're nearly there. Hegai's a friend of mine. He'll make you comfortable as soon as we get there."

Perhaps the situation wouldn't be bad if the other people in the palace were as kind as Otanes, Esther considered. And then the words, repeated to her so often by her father, burned into her

4

consciousness: "The Lord...is a buckler to all those that trust in Him."

No matter what she faced, God would shield her. She squared her shoulders as they entered a side gate, looking for Mordecai. Maybe she would be able to speak to him; maybe he knew these guards and would be able to redeem her. But the sentry who admitted them was not Mordecai.

⌘⌘

At the moment Esther was being escorted onto the palace grounds, Mordecai was listening to a distraught Rachel as she poured out a disjointed story about Esther's capture by palace guards. The teenager, still breathing heavily from her headlong flight, could barely talk. Mordecai, although alarmed about Esther, made Rachel sit down, and Sarah made her breathe into an empty sack. When the girl seemed calmer, Mordecai asked her to begin again.

"Softa Sarah needed herbs because she's been in so much pain lately, so Esther decided to chance a trip to the marketplace. She bought the herbs while I kept a lookout for soldiers. We were almost out of the market when a street boy who had stolen some fruit ran into Esther while trying to get away from the fruit seller. I was a little ahead of Esther, so I didn't know what happened until I turned to speak with her and she wasn't there." Rachel began to wail.

"Two Persian soldiers were helping her off the ground. I watched when they started back through the market, and then Esther looked for me, and one of the guards started chasing me. I stood there, like I was rooted to the spot, watching him come for me until I heard Esther scream at me to run. Otherwise, he would have caught me. It's so awful!" And she broke down completely in sobs.

Sarah stroked her hair, commenting softly, "Praise to the Almighty for giving you fast legs, child. Shhh, now."

"I should have done something," Rachel said, wiping her face.

"Nonsense! What could a little girl like you have done against two armed soldiers? Nothing! I shouldn't have let her venture from home," Sarah answered.

"No one's to blame." Mordecai gave them each a long, steadying look. "We can't control the laws of this heathen country and its king."

"The king already has plenty of women. He uses them up and tosses them away. Oh, Esther!" Rachel wailed.

Sarah swallowed a huge lump in her throat and said quietly, "'He who keeps Israel will neither slumber nor sleep.' He knows what's happened, and He allowed it. He must have a plan for our Esther."

⌘⌘

Sarah had already retired to rest in the other room, and Rachel had left when Ezra appeared on Mordecai's doorstep. "Mordecai, you've heard? My cousin saw the guards hustling Esther through the potter's district. Quickly, let's organize a few men and boys to rescue her."

Mordecai almost smiled. "What do you want, Rabbi Ezra? A war?"

"I want my bride back!"

Mordecai's amusement quickly faded, and he sat down heavily on a three-legged stool. "For a wise man you're playing the fool, my friend. First, Esther's already in the palace by now. Second, she wasn't going to be your bride." Mordecai let his words sink in, then continued, "I couldn't ask for a finer son-in-law than you, but her heart belonged to another."

"Whether Esther would have married me or not, we must rescue her. She's one of us. We'll scale the palace walls at night—"

Mordecai interrupted. "The virgins are guarded day and night. Any rescuers would be killed, and the girls might be harmed."

Ezra fell silent for several long moments. "Are you speaking the truth when you say Esther and I wouldn't have wed? Or are you sparing me pain since I've lost her?"

"I value you too much to offer you lies, my friend."

"And yet I know you to be a man of compassion. I beg you to disclose the name of her intended," Ezra challenged.

Mordecai stared at the wall for several moments before replying thoughtfully, "I think the kindest thing I can do for you is to tell you his name so you can put this matter to rest. Esther had chosen David."

Crestfallen, Ezra nodded and disappeared.

# 2

# A New Life

The courtyard was dazzling. Paths of white marble opened in several directions to fountains springing ten feet into the air. Colored tile mosaics patterned like stars and suns surrounded the fountains. A riot of deep red and purple flowers perfumed the air. Trees, extremely rare in this desert city, abounded, throwing welcome shade over marble and gold benches. A *qanat* in the center of the garden irrigated the entire plot.

Esther's steps had slowed as she gazed at the beauty. Otanes good-naturedly dismissed his companion and allowed Esther to drink in the colors and smells as they passed. But they arrived at an entry to the palace all too soon for Esther, and her mind snapped back to her unenviable position.

Otanes whispered to a servant, who disappeared along a hallway. Several other girls were waiting in an antechamber to which Otanes led her. They were richly dressed and heavily veiled and attended by their own personal servants. Esther looked down at her dusty robes and felt hopeful. Maybe this Hegai would release her because of her bedraggled appearance.

Hegai did not keep them waiting long. He gave Otanes a smile as he entered but greeted the envoys for the waiting beauties first. Rich families had sent their choice daughters with great expectations of culling royal favor. One girl wore Chaldean garments. Another's servants appeared Indian, and yet another towered over her competitors with a height proclaiming she belonged to the mountain clans who lived in the cold northern reaches of the empire.

Esther watched curiously as a chambermaid who had come with Hegai unveiled each one for Hegai's approval. All were accepted, and at last it was Esther's turn. Otanes explained how he found Esther in the bazaar as Hegai appraised Esther's appearance with a slight smile.

"An extraordinary face this one," he said, and since they both spoke Aramaic, gently asked Esther to remove her veil. When Esther complied, he nodded in approval. "Yes, this one the king will definitely wish to see."

Esther's face must have betrayed her disappointment for as Otanes turned to leave, he gave her a quick wink. "Take good care of her, Hegai. She's a true jewel."

"How old are you, child?" Hegai inquired.

"I'll be fifteen in four months."

"I'll arrange a room for you with other women your age. Tomorrow you will be examined by the women's physician. Make yourself comfortable in the suite where the chambermaid will take you."

⌘⌘

Otanes reached his humble one-room home tired and discouraged. He greeted his wife and tousled his six-year-old's hair. His wife brought succulent lamb followed by fresh oranges from one of the few citrus trees in the common courtyard. He automatically offered a prayer for the stability of the empire and the health of the king. But even after eating the delicious meal, he felt drained.

"Was it a difficult day?" his wife, Artystone, asked, as she spun wool in the corner of the room. She knew the king could make all his retainers' lives hellish when he was unreasonable.

Otanes smiled and studied his wife. She was homely, but kind and capable. And thanks be to Ahura-Mazda, she was pregnant with their second child! He could already feel the baby kicking when he touched her rounded belly. Hopefully, it would be another strong son. Then they could think about producing some daughters. May it not require another six years!

"I had to take another contestant up to the palace today."

Artystone knew he never escorted any of the willing girls. They came with their own servants.

"Just a scared slip of a thing. Absolutely ravishing, with dark, wavy hair and big green eyes. Hegai had to accept her. . ." Otanes' voice trailed off sadly. "Poor chit! I'll have to keep inquiring about her, find out what I've done to her future, although I suppose the gods appointed this destiny for her. I wouldn't be surprised if she became our next queen. She has a way about her."

⌘⌘

Mordecai hoped Esther would have the presence of mind to spend time in the gardens near the front gate where he could communicate with her. His mind whirled as he hurried to his duties at the break of dawn. He was early. The other sentries would not expect to be relieved yet, and he should be able to take a quick look for his girl. She was an early riser, and he suspected she had not slept well last night in her new circumstances.

He had decided he could not speak much with her. During the sleepless night, Adonai had impressed on him that Esther must reveal her Jewish blood to no one. He suspected those in the palace would treat her better if they did not think she came from an insignificant race of subjugated people. Of course, he knew he was as good as the Persians and had raised Esther to believe the same.

She had been sheltered from most prejudice since they lived among Jewish neighbors. The little business they transacted with Persian merchants had been established when she was small. Prompt payment had earned their respect long before Esther dealt with them.

Mordecai turned toward the women's quarters after he entered the gate. The sentry allowed him to pass unchallenged after Mordecai assured him he would return shortly to relieve him, well ahead of the scheduled time.

He spotted Esther sitting on a bench facing the sunrise instead of the path he followed. Relieved, he approached her from behind but stopped at a tree a few feet from her bench where he pretended to examine the branches and fruit as a gardener would. "Don't turn, Little Star, but it's me, Father. I need to tell you some important things."

Esther uttered a small cry at hearing the well-loved voice, but she kept watching the sun's rays.

"First of all, your softa and I love you so much, Hadassah." Mordecai's voice caught. He swallowed hard and continued. "I'm sorry this happened to you, but your grandmother and I believe God has His hand in this. You must not reveal your heritage though. It might hurt your chances here."

"I don't care who knows. I don't want to be here."

"But you are here, child. You won't be allowed to leave."

"Oh, Father, I'm so sorry I went to the market."

"It's not your fault, Hadassah. Your grandmother needed those herbs, and I'd been detained at the palace for days. You are part of the harem now, and we must make the best of it. Listen, I can't talk with you any longer. All my comrades know I am a Jew. But I will pass by the windows where the women are kept every day around noon. Softa and I will beseech Heaven for you every day. 'Be strong and courageous. Do not be terrified; do not be discouraged, for the Lord your God will be with you wherever you go.' "

Shoulders drooping, Esther sat and thought about her father's words long after he had gone. Then she rose, lifted her face to the sun, and went inside to take on the challenges of the first day of her new life in the palace.

# 3

# Settling In

As the weeks unfolded, Esther slowly adjusted to the new routine and surroundings. She slept on cushions in a room with four other fourteen-year-olds. Zeina was a petite, dark-haired girl from Lebanon. Princess Anezka was tall, light-skinned, and blond, from the Caucasus.

Mitra also appeared to be a princess, although her roommates weren't sure as they had to communicate with gestures. She wore a necklace of rubies, and two women from her own country waited on her. But she was friendly and liked to listen intently to the other girls. She had already picked up a few words of Aramaic.

Every morning she would walk around the room and point to things. When the other girls would tell her the Aramaic word for cushion or brush, Mitra would repeat it a half dozen times and then go on to another object. After a dozen new words, she would go back and test herself. She rarely missed a word.

The fourth girl, Della, rarely spoke at all. She spent most of her time on her bed of cushions with the gauzy drapes drawn around her for privacy. Other times she gazed sadly out of the window.

Every morning the girls went to the baths on the lower level of the women's house, which was separated from the king's court by part of the garden. Here they soaked for two hours in water tinged with myrrh oil. The young women luxuriated in this bath in two shifts of forty ladies each. This would be their regimen for six months. Then they would spend six months basking in other fragrances. Already there were another eighty girls in this second part of their preparation. Plus the king already had seventeen concubines, not counting Vashti, wherever she was.

Esther's turn at the baths was early in the day. Then she was served fruits and breads on gold platters in the women's dining room. After the meal, she went outside to walk or sit in the shade until it grew too hot. During the heat of the day, she would retreat to the cool stone rooms of the palace and work on the Persian tapestry that Mima, one of the king's concubines, was teaching her as well as many others to sew. Sometimes she would retreat to her room and strum quietly on her harp.

One afternoon Anezka hurried into the bedroom, clearly excited, and asked Esther to follow her. Della didn't even acknowledge them from her post at the window, where she was playing plaintively on a small flute, and the other girls were elsewhere, so Esther donned her veil and followed Anezka curiously. They left the women's houses and set off across the courtyard, Anezka chattering excitedly about the royal horses. Anezka loved horses and had even owned one in her homeland.

In order to reach the stables, they would have to walk the entire distance enclosed by the palace walls. Esther had never been to the other side of the palace enclosure, though the girls were allowed to wander freely. She disliked the idea of meeting any more hostile soldiers, and most of the women stayed near their own quarters and gardens. She had no idea Anezka visited way over there.

The girls crossed in front of the king's *apadana*, where he met with his subjects who brought petitions, and behind the main fountain with its huge stone bull. They had already walked nearly

14

half a parasang. "We still have a long way to go," Anezka said, linking arms with Esther.

They passed quarters for the gardeners, grooms, and soldiers as well as rows of lovely climbing roses before they finally reached the stables.

Evidently, Anezka knew the groom on duty because he nodded to the girls in a friendly way and then continued with his work as though they were not even there.

Anezka made a beeline for a gorgeous bay horse towering over them. She scooped wheat from a nearby bucket and offered the horse an open hand dripping with wheat. The bay hesitated only a moment before prancing toward her and eating the wheat. Anezka slowly brought up her other hand and patted his neck, brushing through his mane with her long, sensitive fingers. All the while Esther hung back, a little frightened of so huge a beast.

When the stallion finished his treat, he trotted to the back of his stall and then outside into a large yard. Anezka turned and explained, "This is one of the king's horses, favored for battle, and, of course, for siring handsome offspring. Come, I will show you the horse I fancy. Perhaps if the king favors me enough, he will let me have a horse."

She led Esther farther into the stables to a stall with a smaller brown mare. She sported a flowing black mane and tail and stepped daintily toward them. Anezka took a piece of fruit from the folds of her robe and caressed the mare's neck and flank as she ate. "She's so gentle. Here, get some grain and you can feed her too. She reminds me of my horse at home."

"Why did you have a horse?" Esther asked as she scooped up some grain. "I thought horses were for hunting and fighting."

"My father saw I loved horses. When I was a little girl, he used to let me ride in front of him on his white charger when he walked Star around the courtyard. Usually only boys learn to ride, but at the time, he had no sons and I was the eldest, so when he saw my interest in horses, he told one of his grooms to teach me to ride."

Anezka's voice softened with affection for her father. "My father was very kind, and life at the palace was much different from here. He has married only two wives. He took a second wife when my mother died bearing her fourth daughter. Fortunately for everyone his second queen bore three sons very quickly. Anyway, all in all, father has only nine children, and he had at least a little time for every one of us...more for his sons, but that's to be expected, don't you think?

"Anyway, when I turned ten, he gave me the magnificent present of a small gray and white gelding. I named her Danika. Danika was just the size of this little lady here. I suspect father gave him to me because he was too small for battle, but all the same it was a lovely present, and I rode him almost every day. How I miss Danika! I wonder who rides him now... perhaps one of my sisters." Anezka's voice trailed off, and Esther knew she was thinking of her home as she absently patted the mare.

"I wish I could have stayed closer to home," Anezka eventually continued. "Of course, I always knew Father would give me in marriage to an important ally or noble, but Susa is so far from home. I miss the lush mountains." She looked at Esther a little sheepishly. "Of course, Xerxes is fabulously wealthy, the richest anywhere and king of an empire. It could be worse. But why are you here, Esther? You've never told us."

"A friend and I went to the bazaar in town to buy herbs for my grandmother. She's been poorly for some time, and while I was there a boy ran into me. He knocked my veil off right in front of two Persian soldiers. They brought me in because of the king's contest."

"So you didn't come because you want to be part of the king's household?"

"Oh, no. There was no way out. When I saw the carefully dressed beauties waiting to meet Hegai, I was hoping he would let me go home because of my bedraggled clothes and hair, but he looked beyond the mess. So much for being beautiful," Esther replied with a wry smile.

16

"You realize you're one of the most beautiful here, don't you, Esther?"

Esther shrugged. "Do you think so? Every girl is so different. You, with your light skin and hair, and the exotic Indian princess. Then there's Isis, with her beautiful black skin and confident poise."

"I don't like Isis. She struts around like she's already queen and everyone else should kiss the ground at her feet. My servant-girl told me Isis' mother wasn't even married to her father. She was gossiping with Isis' black slave one day and the slave told her because Isis had struck her that morning with a mirror. Can you imagine? How ill-tempered!"

Celia continued without pause. "I certainly hope she doesn't become queen or replace Mima as head concubine. She'd make life miserable for all the rest of us.

"And anyway, back to the point. You're much prettier than everyone except perhaps Isis and Sasha. But Sasha hasn't even bothered to learn Aramaic yet. She sits around and mopes most of the day, like Della. I wonder what's wrong with them. They might as well make the best of the situation.

"At any rate, you have a good shot at becoming queen, and I think you'd make a good one. At least you wouldn't lord it over everyone. If you do become queen, could you try to get me a horse?"

Esther laughed. "That's a very big 'if,' but 'if' I become queen, I'll try to get you a horse, if you'll remain my loyal friend."

"Done."

The two smiled at each other. It felt wonderful to have an ally, Esther thought. "I'm not even sure I'd want to be queen. Then everyone's jealousies would be aimed at me."

"Everyone likes you, Esther, except for Isis because she knows you're a threat to her ambitions. She doesn't like anyone except the girls who fawn over her.

"You're right about becoming queen, though," Anezka continued after a brief pause. "Whoever gains the king's favor will be disliked by the others, but I want to be your friend, whether you become queen or not. Promise me the same."

"I promise," Esther vowed, linking her arm through Anezka's. "Let's get back to the women's quarters for the afternoon stories. I like hearing the storyteller strum on his harp and sing about Cambyses, and Cyrus, and the other kings. I've never heard most of those stories before."

"I'd rather hear about Mount Alburz and the smirgh who lives there. Do you think there's really a bridge from the emerald mountain to heaven?"

"No. My people believe we must have faith in Adonai and follow the commands he gave us..." Just then the girls emerged from the stables. Instead of the peaceful summer morning they expected, they encountered pandemonium. Grooms and soldiers were running toward the center of the palace enclave.

# 4

# The Competition Narrowed

**W**hat's wrong?" Anezka asked one of the grooms as he sprinted by with a rope.

"There's a girl in the fountain," he shouted.

Esther and Anezka looked at each other, picked up their skirts, and ran toward the fountain. "Oh, I hope it's not Della," Esther managed to gasp out as they came within eyesight of the fountain and the crowd surrounding it.

Two men were already wading and swimming in the fountain. One of them was on his back, dragging a figure and trying to keep her head above water. When Esther and Anezka saw the flash of red silk, they knew immediately it was Sasha, the unhappy Indian princess.

Her maid ran from the crowd as her mistress was lifted from the pool. The poor girl was wringing her hands and crying hysterically.

One of the soldiers stepped forward and felt for the princess' pulse. "She's dead," he announced with authority.

There were cries from the dozen or so contestants who had gathered. The maid drew a dagger, attempting to plunge it into her heart, but a quick-witted groom caught her arm and a soldier wrested the knife from her grip. She threw herself onto the ground beside her dead mistress, moaning and sobbing.

At this point Tarshish, one of the princes of Media, a close advisor of the king, appeared. "Does anyone know what's happened here?"

A groom stepped forward and said he had been on his way by the fountain when he had seen the princess wading deeper and deeper into the water, as if in a trance. He shouted to her, but she had not responded and had gone under. Unable to swim, he cried for help and ran to the nearest barracks for the soldiers.

Just then Memucan, another princely advisor to the king, descended the steps of the apadana. He and Tarshish consulted together in low murmurs. After a few moments, Memucan dismissed the soldiers, telling two of them to fetch a rock slab to lay the princess' body on. Fearing a reprimand for their curiosity, the grooms had already scattered to their various tasks with the exception of Dar, who had first witnessed the incident.

"Perhaps the maid can tell us something," Tarshish added, pointing to the prostrate form.

"Well, yes, if we can find someone who speaks her dialect," Memucan said, beckoning a servant who had followed him from the apadana. "Go find me an interpreter who knows this woman's language."

The remaining contestants had formed a group under a nearby elm.

"Why do you think she did it?" whispered a wide-eyed thirteen-year-old named Lydia.

"Do you suppose she was drugged? The groom said she looked in a trance," said a second.

"Perhaps someone poisoned her drink," suggested a petite, dark-eyed girl.

"Look, do you suppose that's the interpreter now?" said Anezka, pointing beyond the fountain's glare. "Let's get closer."

Two chambermaids had carried the Indian servant girl to a seat on the side of the fountain away from her mistress. One lifted a cup of wine to her lips as the princes and interpreter faced her.

"Ask the girl what she knows about this," Memucan commanded.

The interpreter fired a question at the girl.

She was still pale and dazed and said nothing.

The interpreter looked questioningly at Memucan and tried again.

Still no reply.

Annoyance crossed the princes' faces. One of the chambermaids gave the girl a sharp shake that seemed to revive her a little. She looked at the interpreter and said something very softly.

He asked her another question.

She shook her head and repeated her first words.

"What's she saying?" Tarshish demanded with a frown.

"She says she must be put to death because she did not take good care of her mistress."

"What nonsense is this?" Memucan asked impatiently.

"It's an Indian custom. The princess Sasha's family must have put the good health of their daughter into the hands of their most trusted female servant," the interpreter replied. He spoke a few words to the girl, who nodded sadly.

"But why would the princess drown herself? Was someone being unkind to her? Is Hegai mistreating some of the girls?" Memucan persisted.

Esther gasped softly when she heard the prince's last question. Hegai was unfailingly kind to all the women in his charge, but the Indian girl was upset. If she said anything at all to impugn him, Hegai would be removed from his position and, in all probability, the king would have him executed.

This time the Indian servant replied with a volley of words to the questions asked by the interpreter.

"She says Hegai treated her mistress extremely kindly, sending delicacies to tempt her appetite and providing as much distraction as possible with the singing poets and musicians. No, her princess was treated royally. She was just very unhappy. She missed her homeland and family, and the girl hesitated to tell me this, Prince Memucan, but from the age of five the princess had been betrothed to an Indian prince. He grew up with her family after his parents died in a plague.

"Although she was only thirteen, they would have been formally married this month. It was driving her out of her mind with sorrow, but the maid never suspected the princess would try to commit suicide. She thought her mistress would feel better eventually."

"She would rather have married some minor prince than the greatest king in the world?" Tarshish asked incredulously.

"Evidently. Though the king doesn't need to hear about it." Memucan gazed imperiously at the small knot of girls gathered nearby.

Under this glare, the young women stepped back and murmured, "No, sir, of course not" and "We needn't make the king unhappy" as they hurriedly escaped to their own quarters. When they'd separated themselves from the sorry scene with a few rows of fruit trees, they slowed.

"How sad!" murmured a Babylonian.

"I'm still not convinced it wasn't foul play," insisted the girl who'd spoken earlier. "Isis would love to narrow the competition. Sasha was incredibly beautiful and graceful."

"We'll probably never know." The dark-eyed girl shrugged.

"Isis is a snake."

"Can you imagine not wanting to be queen of this empire?" asked a fourth girl.

"Yes. I would rather have stayed home in the mountains," said a Lebanese beauty. "Here it's always so hot. And anyway," she lowered her voice, "Vashti didn't do too well, though she was queen. I'd be afraid of the king and his counselors if they were all drunk, too. I suppose she's lucky the king didn't fly into a rage and execute her."

A Persian spoke up. "Killing her would have angered the gods. And it would have strengthened Ahriman. It wouldn't have been good politics either, with her family being so powerful."

Anezka and Esther fell behind the others a little as Anezka paused to pluck a pear. "Esther, you'd better be careful. If Isis did drug Sasha, she might come after you too. You don't have Sasha's grace, but you have something else I can't quite explain." She groped for the right word. "Dignity. Yes! You have a dignity that would be very becoming in a queen."

"As far as I'm concerned, Isis can be the queen. I really don't want the job, remember? Poor Sasha." Esther's face was troubled. "She must have really loved her prince. I wonder if he feels the same way about her. If so, he'll be distraught when he hears about her death, especially if he suspects the cause."

"What do you think will happen to the maid?" asked Lydia, falling behind the others to talk with Esther and Anezka. "Do you think Memucan will follow the Indian custom and execute her? He surely was exasperated with her. Did you see his face when she didn't answer the interpreter? He started turning purple."

"I hope they don't kill her. She couldn't have been expected to mend a broken heart. Only God can do that," Esther replied.

Lydia shot Esther a strange look, but Esther never noticed.

She was already hurrying up the steps to speak with Della.

# 5

# A Heart-to-Heart

When Esther entered her room, she noticed Della had not moved in the hour of her absence. But she must have noticed the stir in the courtyard because she turned toward Esther and raised her eyebrows slightly in a question.

Esther crossed the room to join Della at the window. "Something awful happened," Esther began. "One of the grooms was passing the fountain when he saw Sasha trying to drown herself. He couldn't swim, and by the time he got help, it was too late. The princess was dead. Memucan and Tarshish questioned Sasha's maid about her mistress' death. She was hysterical and said she should be put to death. Evidently, Sasha's well-being was entrusted to her, and she feels she failed."

Esther looked directly into Della's beautiful brown eyes. "She also said the princess was incredibly unhappy because she loved a prince whom she should have married this month in India."

Della turned her gaze to a quiet pool underneath their window. "And you're wondering if the same thing is wrong with me. No, I'm not languishing over some prince."

It was quiet as the two girls contemplated the pool.

Then Esther began gently and hesitantly. "It's just that I'm worried about you, Della. You seem so distant and unhappy. I thought you'd be feeling better by now. We've been here almost three months. I didn't like coming here either, but we should make the best of it."  Della turned and looked at Esther thoughtfully. "I didn't realize you didn't want to be here. Most of the girls seem thrilled to be part of this crazy contest."

"Well I'm not, and neither is Anezka. And obviously Sasha wasn't either."

"Why don't you want to be here?'

"Partly the same reason as Sasha, though I wasn't engaged to a prince. My father, actually not my father but my cousin who adopted me when my parents died in a fire, was choosing a husband for me. I had lots of good offers from fathers who wanted me to marry their sons. One family owns a jewelry shop in Susa. Another trades with the Egyptians and Ethiopians and lives in the finest house I've ever seen, besides the palace of course."

Esther paused and her eyes became dreamy. "And then there was David's family. They're not particularly wealthy, but they're very widely respected in my community. David is eighteen and has always been so kind to me. He's handsome too, with curly dark hair and laughing brown eyes. He loves to laugh and has ever so many friends. You just can't help loving David."

"I take it he was your favorite," Della remarked with a smile. "Do you think your father would have let you marry him?"

"Yes. David is a good man, and my father wanted me to be happy. I think he was trying to figure out a diplomatic way to tell the other families I preferred a poorer man to their rich sons." Esther laughed. Then she sighed. "But I'm stuck here, with no chance of marrying David. Now you know my secret."

Della gazed out the window for so long Esther thought the conversation was finished, but finally Della said slowly. "I'm not interested in any man. I miss my mother, and I'm worried about her. She's expecting a baby soon and wasn't feeling well when I left home. We both begged my father not to send me away at such a crucial time, but he said he had to for the sake of the kingdom. Xerxes is very powerful, and forging an alliance with him is important to our people."

"Do you have other brothers and sisters?" Esther asked.

"No, I'm an only child. My parents have been trying for years to produce a son, an heir to the throne, but my mother became very ill when I was born, and her illness seems to have affected her fertility. She's lost two pregnancies, and a baby girl was still-born.

"I'd thought my parents weren't trying any more until four months ago when my mother told me she thought she was pregnant. I'll never forget her face when she told me, Esther. She looked scared. I'd never seen her like that before.

"Except for the times when she's been ill with the pregnancies, she's the most vivacious, wonderful person I know. We're the best of friends. She's only thirty, and we're more like sisters than anything else."

Della sighed. "My father dotes on her, but it's very important to him to leave an heir. Otherwise, his younger brother's son will succeed him. He and my uncle don't get along at all, and father doesn't like Gerard. He thinks he's vain and impetuous."

"Who's Gerard?"

"He's my cousin who would become the next ruler. To tell the truth, I don't care for him much either. My uncle wanted the two of us to marry, probably to make Gerard's claims to the throne even stronger. We were all appalled. I think that's another reason Father sent me here. He figured anything would be better than marrying Gerard, but I would have married him if it meant I could have stayed near Mother." Della began to sob.

Esther touched her arm gently. "This is a heavy burden, Della. I'll pray for God's protection over your mother."

"I beg the gods for her every day. I ask for a brother, too, but not as much. Mother said she'd send me news through a messenger. I wish I'd heard something by now." Della dried her eyes. "Mother would say it's no use crying. Look for the rainbow following the rain. I suppose part of the rainbow is escaping Gerard. But then we don't know much about Xerxes.

"I've never even met him. Have you?"

"No."

"Do you think he's as bad as the rumors say?"

"Only time will tell," Esther replied as a chill ran down her spine.

# 6

# New Beginnings

Rachel kicked moodily at the dust as she went to the well to fetch water. Although the day had barely dawned, five other girls were already drawing water or waiting for their turns.

"*Shalom*, Rachel," they greeted her as she set down two large jugs.

"Shalom," Rachel mumbled back, trying to calculate how long she would have to wait before she could get home. She and Esther had always met each other and walked together very early, before any of the other girls reached the well.

Rachel would probably miss eating with her family again. Mother would save her some bread, and as soon as she ate she would have to start grinding meal. Maybe she should start bringing her younger sister, Talia. Although young, Talia could carry another small pot and provide company.

Absorbed in her thoughts, Rachel had not noticed the whispering among the other girls, but now she heard Sapphira, the prettiest of the group, say, "She lost her best friend. Of course her mind's not on water."

Since Esther had been captured, Sapphira had become the prettiest girl in the Jewish community. From the snide tone of the remark and the airs Sapphira had adopted, Rachel surmised the girl was not at all sorry about Esther's situation. Bile rose in her mouth. Why couldn't the soldiers have found Sapphira and hauled her to the palace?

"I guess she was too homely for the soldiers to take," she heard from amongst the whisperings. Then all the girls stared at her.

Rachel was spared from a reaction by the girl drawing at the well. "Actually, I heard Rachel *outran* the soldiers. I doubt any of us could do the same."

Rachel looked curiously at her champion. Amaris was the homeliest girl in their community. She had been ill as a young child and now had small scars all over her face and hands. The other girls spurned her, and she quietly accepted their jibes and taunts.

Esther had made the effort to sometimes include her, but Amaris had responded very little. Esther had attributed her reaction to excessive shyness, but Rachel had considered her unfriendly. She was surprised to hear her speak up now and gave her a grateful look.

⌘⌘

A couple of days later, Rachel finished drawing her water and, noticing Amaris' turn was next, waited for her to fill her two pots. They began walking back to their homes together. "Thank you for speaking up for me the other day. I appreciate your kindness."

Amaris just nodded, but Rachel noticed a flush on her cheeks. After a moment, Amaris said, "It's very difficult to lose a best friend, and Esther was wonderful. I hope she's all right."

Rachel was a little confused. She rarely noticed Amaris with anyone else, never mind a constant companion who could be considered a best friend. Yet Amaris' words seemed to stem from personal experience.

As if sensing her question, Amaris said, "My sister died when I was eight. She was about a year older. We both caught that terrible fever. It scarred me, but it killed her and my baby brother. Now it's only me and two younger brothers. I still miss Deborah every day. I know my mother misses all of them." Amaris stopped suddenly as if she had revealed too much.

Rachel said softly, "I'm so sorry. I didn't realize how much your family has suffered."

"A lot of people died in Susa that year. Too many to keep track of unless you knew them personally."

"Yes, my mother's sister died. It was a terrible time."

Outside the gate to Amaris' house, Rachel paused. "Would you like to walk to the well with me tomorrow? I like to go early to avoid the wait."

"I'd like that very much. Shalom, Rachel."

"Shalom, Amaris."

⌘⌘

"Are you ready to go down to the baths, Esther?" Della asked. "I'm going down now."

"Wait. I just need to find my robe," Esther answered, searching through a trunk full of clothing. "Oh, here's one I can use."

"It's beautiful, such a rich purple color. Why don't I remember your wearing it before?" Della asked.

"I usually wear the white one or the red one. The maids must be washing them both today. I really don't care for purple."

"It's the color of royalty, Esther," Anezka said as she joined them.

"You might have to get used to it. Where'd you get it? I love purple."

"Since I arrived with no luggage, Hegai gave it to me, along with all my other clothes."

"He must have his eye on you as a good possibility for the next queen," Anezka commented.

The three young women reached the baths and soaked luxuriously with a brief interlude for massages and cool drinks. After the allotted two and a half hours, they emerged from the warm waters to return to the women's quarters for a light brunch. Anezka and Della were already passing out the doors into the hot sunshine when Esther called them back.

"Wait. Have you seen my robe? I can't find it, and I can't leave the baths like this."

While Della and Esther searched the room where they'd left their robes, Anezka moved on to adjacent rooms. Before they finished, she returned with a knowing expression. "You can stop looking. Some of the other girls saw Isis leave about a quarter of an hour ago. She was wearing a purple robe. I'll bet it was yours, Esther. I say we sneak into her room and take it back this afternoon when she goes for her daily exercise in the garden."

"We don't know it was mine, Anezka. She may very well have her own purple robe. I hear she arrived with a dozen trunks. I'm sure we haven't seen all their glory yet."

"Anyway," Della added, "if she did take it, she wouldn't leave it lying around. And if we did find it, she'd insist it was hers. She'd just say she and Esther must have owned similar robes."

"I still think we should check her room, or we could have our maid look around," Anezka persisted.

"No, no. Let's not cause trouble. It's not like it was my only robe. I'll send Atossa to fetch me another one. Do you have one I can borrow, Della? We're about the same height."

"I have a sea green one that will look marvelous on you. Atossa," Della said, beckoning to the maid who had accompanied them to the baths, "please get my green robe and bring it back here."

"You're too easy-going, Esther," Anezka said. "If you become queen, you'll have to change."

⌘⌘

Rachel found Ezra staring into space outside the door of his family's pottery shop. Not many of the Jews deported to Babylon had adopted this art. Ezra's family was one of the few. Of course, his mother's father had been a potter in *Yehud* before the captivity. His father's line was priestly, which was the reason Ezra spent most of his time at the bet 'amma.

His brothers managed the business, although when he concentrated, Ezra could do beautiful work. But lately, since Esther's capture, he had done little at either the bet 'amma or the shop.

*Such a waste*, Rachel thought to herself. She called his name three times before he even focused on her. "Rabbi Barak needs your help teaching the younger boys today. Joseph has gone home ill."  Still Ezra failed to respond or even move.

Exasperated, Rachel lost her temper, "Wake up, Ezra. Come back to the land of the living. Esther is gone from our lives, but she lives. We both know she will not give up. She's probably counseling half those girls by now. And Softa Sarah says God has a purpose in all this. If a dying old woman can endure her only living grandchild being taken, you and I can too."

A flicker of light brightened Ezra's eyes. "Thank you, Rachel," he said, examining her as though seeing her for the first time. "I'll go see to those five-year-olds. They're always getting into scrapes if left to themselves."

# 7

# An Empty Palace

**W**ord came unexpectedly that the king was moving to Persepolis with a diminished court. No one seemed to know when he would be returning. Favorites from the harem would accompany the king, but it was unclear whether any contestants would be included.

Esther fervently hoped not. Mordecai was able to pass by her window at least once a day around noon before his mid-day rest. They were rarely able to communicate, but she prayed this small comfort would not be taken from her.

Other girls were eager to accompany the king on his summer retreat. Some of them had almost completed their twelve-month beauty regimes. One of the servants, a cousin of Atossa, was fanning the king when the Egyptian ambassador approached him. The envoy suggested the beauties with only a month left to complete be taken along for the king's pleasure.

When the girls heard this news, they figured out twenty of them fell into that category, including Isis. Of course, the ambassador had craftily framed his words to promote Isis and therefore the interests of Egypt. After all, she and Esther were prime candidates, and five months remained in Esther's program.

King Xerxes, happy as always to gratify himself, complied readily with the ambassador's advice. The huge caravan was readied. Every concubine or contestant veiled herself and rode by covered camel. Three of the king's chief counselors and a dozen of his favorite servants rode fine horses, and the king himself led the procession on his bay stallion. A vanguard of four hundred soldiers protected the cavalcade. Most of those left behind at Susa gathered to watch the procession file out of the main gate.

Esther joined the crowd with the hope of exchanging a few words with Mordecai, who usually worked at the main entrance.

She was unable to find him, however, before Anezka found her. "Look, Isis is wearing purple, Esther."

Esther turned as Isis' dromedary passed within ten feet of her. She had parted the dust curtains to bid farewell to Susa, and her cool eyes met Esther's startled ones. She lifted a hand in farewell.

"We couldn't get a good look at her robe," Anezka said in disappointment. When Esther failed to reply, she turned toward her friend, who stood frozen, gazing after Isis.

"I didn't need to. It was mine."

"How do you know?" Anezka asked in amazement. "I thought you were giving her the benefit of the doubt."

"I was, but there's no doubt now. The gold fringe on the left sleeve of my gown was separating from the fabric. I noticed it the day before my robe disappeared. Isis' outfit had the same defect. I noticed when she waved. I think she meant for me to recognize it."

"But why?"

"Because she thinks she's won this contest because she's accompanying the king and I'm not."

"She may be right. Doesn't that bother you?"

"I don't know," Esther said slowly. "If she becomes queen, I certainly don't want her to choose me as her chief enemy."

34

"That could be dangerous to your health. You'd better think of a way to impress the king, Esther. We'd all be a lot better off with you as the next queen."

"I'm not sure what I can do, Anezka, but what's bothering me right now is I can't seem to find Mordecai." She scrutinized the crowd. "I'm going to mingle until everyone leaves."

⌘⌘

Mordecai found Esther about a quarter of an hour later and immediately sensed something was troubling her. "What's wrong, my daughter?"

"Father, I feel like...I'm not sure I can explain it. Scared. Unhappy. I...I feel like I'm walking in slippery places, dangerous places, where if I fall I'll be destroyed."

"It's times like this, my child, when you must cling to God's hand. As King David wrote, 'It is God who arms me with strength and makes my way perfect. He makes my feet like hinds' feet, and sets me upon my high places.' "

⌘⌘

Esther liked the tranquility of the palace after the king's departure. Official business was cut to a bare minimum and handled by two of the king's counselors who lived in Susa. Memucan had left with the king, and Tarshish had returned to the affairs of his province, so Carshena visited the palace every other day to attend to pressing matters. One of the king's new favorites transacted the remaining royal business. He was a handsome, aristocratic Amalekite named Haman.

Esther crossed his path in the garden one day and was unpleasantly surprised to feel his cold, penetrating stare. He might be the king's favorite, but she thought he must have few friends otherwise. He certainly seemed unfriendly toward her. She wondered if he were another potential enemy in this endless political game.

She sighed deeply, sounding, she thought, like an old widow with a multitude of problems. There had been a time when she had no personal enemies. Her people faced many enemies, chiefly the Persians at the present time, but no one had disliked her personally. She thought wryly dislike was too mild a word for Isis' attitude toward her.

Esther had wandered into the cool vault housing the royal scrolls. It was too warm to sit in the garden during the heat of the day. And she needed something new to think about. Mordecai had taught her to read Hebrew. She wondered if any of these scrolls were in Hebrew.

Several scholars were scattered about studying or copying scrolls. Esther chose a secluded corner and began to examine a few of the scrolls. She had not learned how to read Persian. Most of these documents were probably written in Old Persian anyway.

Then her eye caught some familiar letters. Esther unrolled the scroll quickly. She was disappointed to be reading about Nebuchadnezzar's invasion of Yehud, so she tried the scroll next to it. It too was in Hebrew—the words of the prophet Jeremiah. She couldn't believe she had found such a scroll in the king's palace. Why would Hebrew scrolls be here?

She searched eagerly and discovered five scrolls.

⌘⌘

The next afternoon Hegai approached her when she returned from a visit to the stables with Anezka. "I've taken the liberty of appointing a tower room for you. Seven chamberlains will wait on you. They've already removed your possessions from your former room."

Esther was momentarily stunned. The tower rooms were the best rooms in the women's quarters, and evidently she would no longer have roommates. She wondered if she would miss them immensely or prize the solitude.

Even better, she seemed to gain a friend in the palace. Esther found reassurance in the eunuch's friendliness. In Jeremiah's scrolls, she read God had a purpose for Jeremiah before he was formed in the womb. Maybe, just maybe, Adonai was planning to make her the next queen of Persia.

Esther's new maids loved their mistress. She was not a demanding tyrant like some of the other contestants. She treated them with gentleness and respect instead of assuming they were second-class citizens.

Esther returned to the library as often as she could without drawing attention to herself. She could sometimes be alone in the vault if she visited at lunchtime or dinnertime. On those occasions, she copied the Scriptures so she could read them in her room whenever she liked.

The Psalms were a special encouragement to her. David knew what it was like to be in a slippery place surrounded by enemies. Esther discovered the words Mordecai had given her the day the king left: "It is God who arms me with strength and makes my way perfect. He makes my feet like hinds' feet, and sets me upon my high places." She'd known the song since her infancy, but now she clung to its truths in desperation.

When Esther uncovered the scrolls of Daniel, she finally understood why the king's collection included these Hebrew scrolls. Mordecai had told her of the eunuch Daniel, who managed to serve both Babylonian and Persian kings while giving his allegiance to the King of All Kings.

Over the next few days, she studied these scrolls carefully. It was a little confusing, but Daniel had dreamed of beasts representing kingdoms. God had revealed to him the Medo-Persians would be defeated by another great kingdom. She was surprised the king kept this part of Daniel's writings, but God was preserving His word.

Perhaps God would even use her in this palace, as He had used Daniel over one hundred years ago before other heathen kings. But Daniel had faced great peril, as David had. Esther shuddered at his account of being thrown into the lion's den.

"God, please use me here, like you used Daniel. I want to honor You as he did. I don't understand why I'm here, but please arm me with strength. And please, don't let the king throw me to the lions."

# 8

# The Revelation

The king returned amid trumpet fanfare and bustling preparations. Once again the palace became more formal and busier with official business. The girls left in Susa during the king's absence began their one-night encounters with the king. Several of them even dared to whisper of Xerxes' difficult temperament.

The day after Della's opportunity with the king, Esther visited her in her new quarters. After Sasha's death, Della had shown more vivacity and interest in palace life, although she continued to grieve over her fate. But Esther was unprepared for the broken-spirited girl she found. The two retreated to a quiet corner where there was no danger of being overheard.

"Esther, it was awful. He was in such a foul mood. I couldn't do anything to please him. He kept swearing at me and insulting me. I didn't understand half the words he used, but I got a good idea of his opinion of me. I hope I never see him again. I certainly don't think he'll call for me." Della sobbed. "I've let my father and the kingdom down."

Esther gently squeezed her arm in sympathy, but Della winced. "What's wrong? Let me see your arm." And she caught Della's wrist when Della tried to shrink away.

"It's nothing, nothing."

Esther lifted the flowing sleeve of Della's white gown and gasped when she saw four purple bruises—the imprint of a man's fingers.

"Della, did he leave marks anywhere else?"

"Yes, but I don't want to frighten you."

Esther's eyes were already shining with fear and tears. "Come to my quarters later. I'm sure one of the maids knows something to ease the soreness and perhaps lessen the blemish. You don't think any of the marks are permanent, do you?'

"No, no, and I will visit you. I don't want any of the other concubines—" Della almost choked on the word—"to see these." She tried to smile reassuringly. "I'll come later. Right now I have to arrange my little room."

Esther watched her hurry away. Was she imagining stiffness in her friend's gait? She swallowed a sob, and fled down a staircase. "Help us all," she whispered in prayer.

Sleep eluded Esther that night. Whenever she closed her eyes, she saw Della's pain-filled eyes or bruised arm.

Her maid Parmys had doctored Della's bruises with a soothing herb poultice while Esther was taking her customary afternoon walk. Della had come for the proffered help when she knew Esther would be absent.

Although Esther wondered aloud about the extent of the damage, she could not coax any further information from Parmys other than "her body will heal." Esther deduced Parmys shared her concern for Della's fragile spirit.

As she gazed from her tower window over the moonlit gardens, Esther's thoughts flitted from concern for her friend to anxiety over her upcoming encounter. Why, oh why, couldn't she be at home dreaming of nuptials with David? Why would El Elohim who had protected and led her fathers have allowed her, a helpless woman, to be forced into a pagan king's bed? She dropped her head into her arms and cried softly.

Words of the prophet Jeremiah filtered into her consciousness: "I know the plans I have for you…plans to give you hope and a future." Did God have a plan for her? Yes, He must.

"Sovereign God, you are in control of all things. You call the stars by name and can number the grains of sand on the shore. Please, please help me to do whatever it is You would have me to do here. And heal Della's heart. Help her to receive good news from home."

Feeling more peaceful, Esther finally drifted into a dreamless sleep.

⌘⌘

When Esther was sewing with Mima the next day, Della danced into the room. "Come for a walk with me, Esther. I have good news."

As the girls entered the women's rose garden, Della continued, "A messenger from my mother arrived today. She bore a healthy baby boy four months ago. The entire kingdom is rejoicing, and mother had nearly recovered when the messenger left two months ago. He was captured by bandits in the mountains and held for over a month before he could escape." Tears streamed down Della's radiant face. "Oh, Esther, how I wish I could go home!" Esther wrapped an arm around her and squeezed her affectionately as they walked toward a stone bench.

Maybe, if she gained enough influence with the king, she could somehow return Della to her family. It would not be easy, but she could try. Reportedly, the king lavished his favorites with generosity.

Since returning from Persepolis, the king had called for Isis' company on several occasions. She sported a thick, costly golden necklace and resided in a luxurious private apartment in the concubine's quarters. Evidently, she had pleased the king immensely.

The other forty girls in the first group of contestants had not fared well. Only one or two had been called for a second night with the king. The Lebanese girl often danced for him, and Lydia played the tabrets in his presence. But otherwise, they were largely forgotten.

After one meeting with the king, most of them were relieved. Xerxes was not known for his kindness, and several, like Della, had experienced his wrath.

Meanwhile, the king was working his way through the second wave of beauties. Esther's turn could come any day.

⌘⌘

Rachel felt she would burst with happiness as she turned in the darkness to face her groom of one day. In the moonlight she could just see his peaceful features as he slept beside her.

She had loved Ezra from afar for years, but he had been enamored by Esther's perfection and never seemed to notice her leggy, clumsy friend. Of course, Esther had eyes only for David from the time she was eight years of age and he had rescued her from a fire that had killed several shoppers in the bazaar. Esther had been the only one who knew Rachel's secret, for Rachel had never even hoped for an offer of marriage from the distinguished Levite.

But Ezra had finally noticed her the day she became angry with him. She had dragged herself home and spent days in misery, chastising herself for saying far too much. It was just that it hurt her to see him waste his potential and he had been doing nothing for months.

Then one evening he appeared with roses for her in an exquisite vase he had made himself. For the first time she had allowed herself to hope she might become his help-meet. But he failed to return for over a week, and she convinced herself the gift was only gratitude for her help in lifting him from his despondency.

When he did return, he seemed energized again. As they walked, she told him he seemed more like his old purposeful self again. He looked at her, then replied, "More purposeful, actually."

That evening Rachel told her mother she preferred *Abba* hold off on considering any marriage offers quite yet. A Jewish farmer had been speaking to her father about an engagement. Her mother was happy to agree. Although Rachel was a strong girl, her mother preferred to think of her as a city wife close by, not working hard in the fields outside Susa.

Her parents were both thrilled when Ezra proposed a betrothal only two months later. Once motivated, he was a decisive fellow. It was only the motivating that took so long, Rachel thought.

Just three months later, they were married. Ezra's father had presided over the small but beautiful wedding ceremony. About fifty relatives had attended, along with a small number of close friends, including Amaris.

Rachel was grateful for Amaris and her friendship. Rachel and Esther had planned as children to help each other prepare for their weddings, but God had decreed otherwise.

Amaris had helped Rachel prepare the new home which the young couple was renting from Persians who had moved out of the neighborhood as more and more Jews relocated there. They had carefully set the cookware and water jugs Ezra had fashioned on a couple of wooden benches and the table. The crockery was simple but elegant, far prettier than most other brides'.

When Rachel added the blankets she had been weaving for years in preparation for her nuptials, the two rooms became a very cozy place. Amaris declared the effect perfect and laughed when Rachel wondered aloud if Ezra would notice because he always seemed to be thinking of things unseen.

Then the two had held each other and cried. Amaris confided she hoped Rachel would help her set up house someday.

Rachel knew her friend's unspoken thoughts. Perhaps no man would offer for her or, if a poor farmer outside the city did pay her family a dowry, Amaris might need to relocate far from the city. Rachel assured her she would find a wonderful husband.

Rachel's thoughts turned to her other friend. She hoped Esther had found friends in the palace.

# 9

# Esther's Turn

Hegai himself arrived in her quarters one evening. "Come—tonight it is your turn. Let's get you ready." In a high state of excitement, he began sorting through her clothes while her maids undressed, washed, and perfumed her.

He settled on a jade-colored robe with delicate thongs for her feet and bangles for her wrists. Parmys painted her face and nails. Then Atossa swept her hair upwards into gold hair clasps, and Hegai twirled her around to study the effect and decide if any other touches were necessary.

"Beautiful," he pronounced. "And now, my little jewel, smile, relax. The king is in excellent spirits, having received favorable news about his troops. Why don't you take your harp and play a bit as the king enjoys a light repast? Music should relax you and create a mood. Our hopes go with you. I know you'll not let us down," he added with an encouraging smile.

At the entrance to the king's private quarters, Esther paused and took a deep breath, whispering, "God of my fathers, help me." Then she plunged through the door and into her future.

The king was eating with great gusto. With a smile and interest lighting his eyes, he motioned her to a golden seat on his right. Esther found the courage to meet his silent scrutiny by studying him a bit and then suggesting she play for him.

She found it easier to busy herself with the strings of her familiar harp than to try to meet or ignore his gaze. When she did glance up from time to time, she noted the king looked delighted. She relaxed. Feeling peaceful, she sang softly to some of the tunes until the king bade her to join him for some wine.

She slowly sipped one glass as they gazed over the king's private gardens, which wafted delicate perfumes into his dining area, but refused a second. Then the king bade her dance.

She was becoming increasingly thankful Mima and Hegai had instructed her in Persian music and dance. Otherwise, she would only have known Jewish songs and steps. She would have either needed to refuse or reveal her race. Still, it couldn't hurt to slip a Hebrew performance in once in a while. She could even bring her tambourine to dance to.

Presently, the only music accompanying her was the jingle of her bangles. *Listen to me. I actually expect the king to ask me back.* She glanced at him as she whirled. He certainly looked pleased.

Actually encountering the king was a shock, especially since he was incredibly gentle. Afterwards, she was considering slipping away since the king appeared to be sleeping, but when she moved to don her robe, she heard a faint, "Stay a bit longer."

So she gave him a massage instead. She had become adept at massage while attempting to alleviate her grandmother's painfully sore muscles. Before long, the king was in a deep, comfortable sleep with the hint of a smile softening his face, and Esther returned to her tower room.

⌘⌘

The next morning, the king sent for Memucan before he finished breakfasting. "You've been taking note of the virgins in the palace, I presume?"

"Yes, sire," Memucan responded with a bow.

"What is your assessment of the one with the unusual green eyes, the one called Esther?"

"Very lovely, sire. Besides this, she carries herself in a dignified manner without exuding the haughtiness of some of her rivals."

"Ah, you mean Isis particularly. Yes, she is a proud filly, but such a challenge." The king's eyes gleamed. "I understand you counselors do not wish her for a queen. She would be a tyrant, though a stunning one. An alliance there could also mean a better relationship with the Egyptians, who are, after all, still powerful. But we were speaking of Esther. What of her family?"

"She has no royal blood. She's from Susa. As for Egypt, your brother Achaemenes seems to be in solid control."

"Still, Isis is the daughter of one of the most influential priests of the land. Solidifying loyalties is always wise."

"Perhaps. But you don't want another Vashti, sire." Memucan noted the troubled look in the king's eyes on an otherwise impassive face and knew he had overstepped.

"I don't think that will be a problem, after the example I made of Vashti."

"No, sire," Memucan quickly agreed.

"Observe this Esther carefully over the next few days. I think I may be close to naming the new queen."

Memucan turned to go. "And tell Hegai to send up any other especially good prospects nightly for the rest of this week. We'll see if there's anyone else even worthy of consideration."

The king's quarters were very busy the next few days. The king was delaying or delegating other business in order to choose his next queen. The few remaining contestants came and went from his quarters. The king was not impressed with them. The servants and counselors noted he spent hours wandering in the gardens with his brows furrowed in thought.

When this fact was communicated to the harem, the girls quickly guessed who the chief contestants were. Isis conducted herself with her customary haughtiness and gathered a train of admirers who assured her she could never lose to the reserved Esther. Isis had been born a queen, they said.

Other concubines favored Esther, though not as loudly. If Isis should become queen, there was no benefit in incurring her wrath. She would make life miserable enough without anyone's earning special disfavor.

Esther tried to keep her regular schedule as if nothing unusual were going on, but it was almost impossible with all the whispering and servile fawning by harem members and servants alike. Only Anezka and Della remained her unaffected friends.

One evening she and Della arrived in the dining room together to join the others at the long golden table. Immediately the Phoenician and Syrian girls exchanged their seats at the foot of the table to allow Esther and Della to sit at the end with Anezka.

Isis had already established herself at the head of the table with her entourage, so the two beauties were facing each other, one with darkly glowing skin and mysterious violet eyes set perfectly in her proud face, the other with dark hair softly curling above her thoughtful green eyes and gentle smile.

Dinner conversation abruptly ended. Isis broke the tension, rising with two wine goblets in her bejeweled hands and approaching Esther in an uncharacteristically friendly manner.

She handed a golden goblet decorated with lions to Esther. "To the next queen." She lifted her cup in a toast. Esther lifted hers too and pretended to drink but did not swallow any wine. Her stomach was in knots. Something was not right about this superficial kindliness.

48

Isis smiled coldly and returned to her seat. The servants began bringing in trays laden with fruit and others with fish.

As soon as the normal chatter began, Anezka's hand closed on the goblet, and a moment later she surreptitiously spilled it on the floor.

She then called a servant to wipe up the mess.

Esther and Della looked at her in surprise. "What...?" Della began.

Anezka shook her head curtly. "Did you drink any of it?" she hissed.

Esther shook her head.

"Good. I'll explain later."

The trio returned to Esther's tower after the meal. She was the only one of the three who enjoyed private quarters. "What was that all about, Anezka?" she asked. "It didn't feel quite right, but for once Isis was making a show of being nice."

"Nice." Anezka snorted. "A lioness robbed of her cub would be nicer. She put something into the cup she gave you. I watched her pour a powder into it from a vial she brought into the dining hall. At the time I figured it was some type of aphrodisiac, but I noticed she poured it into the lion goblet because she had another goblet with a bull on it. She drank from the bull cup. She was very careful to hand the tampered one to you."

Esther felt a cold chill.

Della gasped. "Do you think she was trying to kill you?"

"I doubt it," Anezka answered. "She's too smart for that. People would have their suspicions. It was probably something to make you sick. She's already had a night with the king this week. She figures the king will want to see Esther again too. If you were too sick to go...." Anezka looked at Esther and shrugged.

Esther finished the thought for herself. "The king might just make her queen."

Della looked worried. "That Isis is horrid. What else do you think she'll try?"

"Hopefully that was her ace. The king will announce Esther as the next queen soon. That should discourage Isis from her tricks, at least for a while. Meanwhile, my dear," Anezka said, turning to Esther, "I think you should stay in your room. If you want to go anywhere, call for me or Della, and we'll take a chambermaid along for extra protection. And, by the gods, be careful what you eat and drink. Perhaps you should have a word with Hegai."

Esther spent most of the week in her tower room, studying her copies of the scrolls Daniel had penned seventy years earlier, trying to remember the Psalms her father and grandmother had taught her. She struggled against the icy fear of Isis' becoming queen. "'Preserve my life from the fear of the enemy. Hide me from the secret counsel of the wicked,'" she prayed again and again.

But the alternative appeared little better. Could she ever please the imperial Xerxes? And if she did, would he eventually abuse her as he had Della? Or dethrone her like Vashti? Why had she ended up in this crazy contest instead of being able to remain at home and marry David?

*Oh God, please deliver my soul.*

# 10

# The New Queen

Hegai arrived at Esther's room early on the last day of the week. "The king wishes to see you," he said, hunting through her gowns for an especially becoming one.

Esther's head spun. Surely this could mean only one thing—the king had chosen her. She had won the contest! She had beaten Isis! In spite of her fears, she was relieved Isis would not be promoted to the head of the harem. She would have made life intolerable.

By the time she reached the apadana to find the king and his council awaiting her arrival, she sparkled with victory and had never appeared more lovely. She approached the king's throne with a proper air of deference and knelt before him.

Xerxes rose from his throne and took her by the hand. "Princes of Media and Persia, swear allegiance to the next queen of this vast empire. On the first day of Adar, we will hold a celebration in honor of our new queen. We will introduce her to the people of Susa and to any other subjects who can be present. Send the couriers to any lands within ten days' distance with invitations to the feast. Make the preparations for a month's celebration in honor of our new queen."

Esther heard his words through a haze. She couldn't believe she was going to be a queen—and of the most powerful realm in the world. Then her thoughts snagged on one of the king's words— feast. Vashti had been deposed because she failed to obey the king's command to appear before drunkards at one of his feasts. Would the king give her a similar command?

The king motioned with his hand, and Memucan appeared at his side with a bag embroidered with mythical figures and gods. The king reached inside and drew out a heavy gold necklace with a huge emerald in its center. Esther remained kneeling as the king fastened it around her neck. This necklace was her symbol of position, for only a Persian queen had the right to wear it. Esther had heard of the necklace, but was surprised at its weight on her neck as well as its incredible beauty.

Next the king drew a crown similarly wrought in gold with emeralds. But she almost gasped aloud when she saw Xerxes remove a large pair of gold and emerald earrings from the bag.

Since the court musicians were playing loud fanfares, the king was able to speak without anyone but Memucan and Esther hearing. "I ordered my finest jeweler to make these for my next queen, Esther. Little did I know they'd match your eyes so perfectly. Wear them in health and happiness."

Then the king raised her by the hand, and all the nobles and servants in the great hall bowed. Only Esther and Xerxes were left standing.

⌘⌘

Esther chose to keep her tower room. She could gaze at the profusion of roses and placid pools from her two tall windows. She was also close to the rest of the harem, so it was easy for Anezka to visit, not that distance would be a problem for Anezka, Esther reflected with a smile.

She also retained her loyal servants with several additions. A guard was posted by her door at all times. Four guards shared this task, so Esther became familiar with all of them.

She was fondest of Otanes, who had brought her to the palace a little over a year ago. He still considered her safety his special commission. Esther was sure Hegai had appointed him for this reason. Otanes must have inquired after her during the long, uncertain months of the contest. Esther was no longer under Hegai's care, but he still looked after her comfort and sent delicacies and baubles for her enjoyment.

But the best change in Esther's retinue was the addition of a special companion. About six weeks after she became queen, the king inquired if she would like anything at all, up to a third of his kingdom. Esther's beauty and demeanor had dazzled all his subjects at her celebration. The king thought she had behaved very well and was delighted with her.

Esther was pleased too, and relieved nothing untoward had occurred. God had protected her. Therefore, she was bolder than usual.

"If it pleases your majesty, may I have one of the women of the harem as a special companion? You haven't called for her since her contest turn." Esther knew many of the women were unlikely to be recalled. They would live out their days, childless, as part of the harem.

"What is the name of the one you'd choose?" the king inquired.

"Della of Sipylus, sire."

"I don't recall her," the king said, with a furrowed brow, trying to remember. She must not have provided a memorable evening. "Your wish is granted, Queen Esther."

Esther's spirits soared in praise to Adonai as she left for the concubines' quarters. Della would be so relieved. She lived in fear the king would call her. Now she could stop worrying. Maybe she would become less homesick. Perhaps one day Esther would even be able to quietly send her home. She would not mention it to Della, but she would look for her chance.

⌘⌘

Artystone adjusted the weight of the heavy rug as she passed the palace gates. Her oldest son came close behind, keeping the rug from dragging in the dust and bearing a little of the burden. She looked curiously toward the palace enclave, wondering what it would be like to be one of the pampered harem within.

Otanes had told her of the new queen's coronation amidst the council. He had been one of the guards. The king had given her jewelry worth more money than Artystone would ever see in her lifetime.

Otanes guarded the queen most of the time he was working. He must have been given extra duties at the palace last night because he had said he would deliver this rug, but he had not returned home.

The rug's new owner would be angry if it were not delivered on time. She was one of the most demanding customers Artystone wove for, but she ordered elaborate rugs of excellent material and paid well, so Artystone did not want to lose her business. Fortunately, she did not live far away.

As Artystone and her son waited for the mistress of the house in a small, cool foyer, Artystone looked around at the beautiful mosaics. Who decided fate—this woman living in opulence while others went hungry?

Why were some people born to a life of ease while most lived in poverty? Her own family did not live in dire poverty, but they were not exactly comfortable either. She and Otanes both worked very hard to provide the basics for the family. Many Persian families did not even have enough to eat, but the gods seemed to bless a few families with abundance. What did the rich do to earn such favor?

Her train of thought broke off as Zeresh swept into the room. Artystone felt awkward and ugly before the perfectly coiffed Zeresh. She was sweaty and disheveled from hauling her handiwork, but Zeresh immediately began to examine the rug Artystone had already spread on the floor without acknowledging the weaver. After a thorough inspection, she nodded as if pleased and handed a small bag of coins to Artystone. "Did you carry this here?" she asked, as if noticing Artystone for the first time.

"Yes."

"What happened to the man who usually delivers the rugs?"

"My husband works at the palace and had to remain there last night."

"Next time send your son with a message that the rug is ready and one of my servants will pick it up at your home," Zeresh said, not unkindly. "It's well done," she added, regarding the rug with pleasure.

⌘⌘

Ezra lifted her right off the floor and nearly began to swing her around like he did with the children at bet 'amma, when he caught himself and carefully set her down, patting her belly. "May you be as fruitful as the wives of Jacob!" he exulted. "When will the baby arrive?"

"Around wheat harvest, I expect," said Rachel, eyes shining. She had not realized he would be so happy to have children. The Almighty was blessing them abundantly. They would only have been married a year when the little one arrived.

# 11

# The Triumph of Isis

Have you heard the news?" Anezka asked as she plopped down on a purple cushion.

"I hear a lot of things. Can you be more specific?" Esther replied, slightly annoyed. Anezka kept up on all the court gossip, which seemed a waste of time to Esther. Most of it ended up being untrue anyway.

"I guess no one's told you, or you'd know exactly what I'm talking about. Isis is pregnant again." Anezka watched her friend closely.

"Oh," Esther said in a deflated tone, sinking down next to the window. Why couldn't she bear the king a child? She spent as much time with him as Isis. The contestants had borne him fifteen sons and twelve daughters. Plus five concubines were presently with child. Well, six now, including Isis. And Isis already had one son.

"Your time will come, Esther," Anezka said in a surprisingly gentle tone.

"How do you know?"

"Because I know your God is looking out for you."

*I've magnified the one true God in Anezka's eyes, so she believes in His power more than I.* Esther smiled at her friend. "I hope and pray you're right."

⌘⌘

Isis began strutting around the palace sporting a necklace disconcertingly like the one the king had given Esther when he announced her as the next queen. Isis' was smaller, true, but the chain was more cunning, for it was a dragon with an emerald in its mouth. Esther heard all about it from her maid Atossa, who was friendly with one of Isis' servants.

"If I may offer a suggestion, my queen...perhaps you should wear your necklace and tiara more often to keep her in her place," Atossa added. Esther always wore the earrings the king had given her at her coronation, but her only other adornment was her mother's headdress.

Esther wondered where her place was, and if it would change if Isis bore a son.

The Persian kings fancied sons. Xerxes often talked of a general son who would defeat the Greeks.

Oh, why couldn't she have a son? She would teach him to be a good king for the benefit of everyone. What good could she possibly do as queen unless she bore an heir to the throne and taught him to be just and temperate, unlike his ancestors? Why didn't God hear her prayer? Why couldn't she share Anezka's faith?

And now Atossa thought she should give up her mother's headdress, too. Esther loved it for its intricacy and connection with her long-dead mother, but she knew the glass beads were common. Many women outside the palace wore them.

It was a very long week. Esther found she could not concentrate on either Daniel's scrolls or her harp. She spent long hours wandering in the hot gardens or gazing over the pools, trailing one hand in the water. Her two bodyguards suffered nearby, but she had failed to notice their discomfort, until today when a maid who followed her with a fan fainted in the sweltering heat. Esther was displeased she had not considered her servants and promptly withdrew to the cooler palace where she cared for the over-heated girl herself.

It was nearly time to prepare for tonight's banquet. The king required her presence at an intimate dinner party for eight in celebration of the noble Haman's birthday. Esther did not care much for the haughty Haman, and she did not wish to entertain in her present state of mind. She could send a message she felt unwell. But no, she sighed, that wasn't exactly the truth. She must of course attend.

She chose a light peach robe and told Parmys to fasten the emerald necklace around her neck. With a pang, she set aside her headdress, and Parmys arranged the diadem in her wavy locks. She personally attached the king's earrings and pinched her cheeks for a bit of color. She was still the queen, for tonight at least, and she must look like it.

Perhaps, if she were beautiful and charming enough, the king would call for her, and she would gain another chance to bear a child. Yes, she must appear vivacious and attract the king's attention. She wondered what Haman's wife would be like. She would soon find out.

Zeresh was nearly as insufferable as her husband. She even walked as though she were the most elegant woman in the party, which was far from the truth. She was pretty and well dressed in a white linen robe complementing her dark features, but Esther easily outshone her, and she knew Herah would too.

Herah, the wife of Prince Memucan, always appeared stunning and aristocratic. She spoke and acted with such taste Esther had watched and emulated Herah in her first months as queen. Herah noticed the younger woman's admiration and tactfully encouraged her with kind words and occasional advice. Esther knew she would always be grateful.

Herah greeted her with a warm smile and deep curtsey this evening. She was dressed in a royal blue that made her eyes shine like the sapphires in her jewelry. She certainly knew how to dress, Esther admitted, and stole a look at the king. She knew how he liked a beautiful woman, but to her surprise he was looking at her in admiration. She relaxed and returned his smile.

The group feasted on a rice dish flavored with Indian spices and chunks of fish. There were succulent oranges and rich dates followed by a superb honeyed confection Esther had never tasted. Herah told her it was bakla, a Greek dessert.

Esther settled back on her couch contentedly. Of all the rooms in the palace, besides her tower suite, she most liked the king's private dining room. Its high ceiling allowed air from the gardens to circulate and cool the guests. From the balcony, she could throw crumbs to the exotic birds enjoying the largest garden pool. Inside, purple linen draped the walls, and an exquisite carpet depicted the duel of a dragon and lion in purple, red, and blue.

Esther had been so intrigued by this rug she had enlisted Mima's aid and worked a dozen pillows with the dragon and lion motif. The king had seemed pleased with the gift. Her pillows lay on the gold couches around the low table.

She fingered the pillow she leaned upon. This one was slightly different from the rest. Unbeknownst to anyone but herself, she had stitched a small star in the upper right-hand corner to remind herself the God of Israel was above all else in heaven and earth. She could gather courage from it when she ate in the presence of this earthly king and his guests.

*God is watching over me, just as He watched over and kept David from his enemies, be they giants or his own sons.* Esther felt peace seeping back into her being.

Haman was bragging about the progress of his youngest

son's riding lessons. He thought Vajezatha would become a better rider than most of his nine brothers, with the exception of Parshandatha. From previous soliloquies by Haman, Esther knew his eldest son, Parshandatha, was his favorite.

Zeresh and his other wives had borne three daughters before the long-awaited son arrived. Parshandatha was a teenager and sometimes accompanied his father to the palace. He had assumed his father's superior air, except with the king, whom he served obsequiously.

Esther glanced at Zeresh to see how she reacted to Haman's opinions about Vajezatha, who was not her son. Zeresh caught her inquiring gaze, seemed to guess its intent, and settled back on her couch. When Haman paused, she added, "May Ahura-Mazda grant the king and queen many sturdy children, like the eight he has granted my husband and me."

Esther colored and looked down at her plate, pushing the last few mouthfuls aside. How had the woman guessed her vulnerability regarding motherhood? The remark, although spoken politely, had not been meant kindly.

Esther looked up miserably to see how the rest of the company was reacting. Herah's sympathetic eyes met hers. Everyone else was looking toward the king. He seemed to sense no affront. "Perhaps in his time, Zeresh. I have many fine sons and daughters, but only one beautiful queen. Perhaps her life should not be risked in childbearing. A true queen is a rare find."

Esther nearly choked in amazement. The king had never praised her in such a way before. Although raw from her own frustration and Zeresh's unkindness, Esther's heart was eased by the king's words.

The group enjoyed the court minstrels and a new poem in Haman's honor, and broke up around midnight. Haman was helped away in his drunken euphoria by two servants. The rest were sufficiently steady to leave under their own power.

Neither Herah nor Esther had drunk much, and the first clasped Esther's hand as she left. After all had departed, Xerxes softly called for Esther from the balcony. Esther was surprised since she thought he had left for his own bedroom, and shocked when she realized he was not even slightly drunk. As a rule, the king enjoyed his wine as much or more than his guests.

The king reached for her waist with one hand and tipped her chin up toward him with the other. "I think that woman's words bothered you, my jewel. Esther, you're of more worth to me as a queen than you would be as the mother of my child. I already have thirty children, but their mothers could never fill your place." Then he smiled. "But come with me tonight."

⌘⌘

Three weeks later Esther knew she had not conceived. She looked out the tall window at the night stars and was comforted anyway.

# 12

# Assassins in the Palace

About a month later, Mordecai sent her a note through her chamberlain, Hatach. The terse note sent a chill down Esther's spine. "Meet me at noon at the south qanat."

What could be wrong? Even when Sarah had died, Mordecai had not sent for her. He had found her in the crowd at the Feast of Midwinter because he did not want to put such news into a note. Sarah had died three weeks before then.

Sadness filled Esther at the thought of losing her softa. She had not even said good-bye the day she left to buy herbs in the bazaar. Sarah had been sleeping, and Esther had never returned to the house. Five years had passed since that fateful day.

Esther looked down at her purple linen dress and wondered what her grandmother would think of her. At least she had improved her skill on the harp. Sarah always said Esther failed to practice enough. How could she with a household to supervise and an invalid on her hands? Sarah understood, but she always sighed, averring Esther could be a superb harpist, if she ever had the chance.

In the palace, Esther had no daily work, so she had ample time to sharpen her skill. Perhaps in the hereafter God would grant her the opportunity to play for her grandmother.

Esther's attention returned to the present as she reread the missive. She paced her quarters until time to leave. Mordecai had chosen a time and place when they would be unlikely to be observed. The secrecy augmented Esther's nervousness.

When she approached the qanat at noon, she was relieved to see Mordecai.

No one else was around. Esther had seen only one guard and a stable boy since she had left the palace. Still, Mordecai could not embrace her or clasp her hand. It would seem highly irregular for a doorman to touch the queen in such a manner to anyone who might glimpse their meeting. Esther paused at a stand of fruit trees and plucked a pear. She then pretended to wish for one beyond her grasp. Immediately Mordecai was by her side to reach the desired fruit.

"Quick thinking, little one," he said with a smile as he offered her the pear. "I always said you were a smart one."

Esther smiled briefly. "What's wrong, Father? Your note worried me."

"Two of the chamberlains are planning to assassinate Xerxes. I couldn't put the information in a note because there are spies all over the palace. I don't know if anyone's involved in the plot besides Bigthan and Teresh. Barnazabus, Teresh's servant, brought me word of it."

"Do you know when the attempt will take place?"

"No. He only heard a small part of the conversation. They were unaware Barnazabus was resting in the gardens as they strolled by talking of their plans. Are you going to see the king soon?"

"Yes, at a small dinner tomorrow evening. Will that be soon enough?"

Mordecai thought for a moment. "I think so, Little Star. Considering the alternative, I think you can safely wait without jeopardizing the king's life."

Esther knew Mordecai was remembering the news from last week. An unbidden magus had approached the king with what he claimed was an important message.

The king had been sitting in his apadana in a black mood, having expressly forbidden the doormen to admit any whom the king had not commanded to appear before him. No one could imagine why the magus had pushed his way through the guards after having been told of the king's directive.

Everyone in Xerxes' kingdom knew approaching the king uninvited resulted in immediate death, except if the king held out his heavy golden scepter. Supplicants could gather outside the apadana and report their business to the scribes, who then reported to the king. He chose to hear some petitions and ignored or delegated the remaining issues. Of course, the king would not give mercy when his explicit command had been ignored.

Esther thought the man's message must have been urgent for him to risk his life. The king thought otherwise.

Once the priest had stammered out his claim to have important information, the king silenced him and commanded the man endure the test for truth. The magus was stunned into silence.

The palace gossips said the test was the king's acknowledgement of the priest's status. Otherwise, he would have been dispatched immediately by the axmen who lined the stairs to the king's throne.

The king chose to test the priest by fire, and arrived at the evening ceremony in better humor. Esther had been summoned to his side, and the king explained if the priest passed the test, the message which he would then impart would receive the king's full attention. If the priest died in the attempt to pass the trial, then he had been lying all along.

Esther watched in horror as the poor man stood before two lines of fire less than a cubit apart. The lines stretched for two hundred feet. His task was to run between them and survive. It was impossible. She was filled with horror that Xerxes would torture a subject in this way. But when she saw the king's profile, she realized not only would he treat the man this way, but derive satisfaction from it.

Her heart was sickened even before the priest became a living, screaming torch halfway through the test. His agony ended when he fell into the flames. The stench lasted longer than the "trial."

Esther had fought back tears and nausea as the king announced, "He was a liar." The royal party turned away. Esther wondered if the ministers and concubines felt as sick as she. She had never seen such cruelty. And the man perpetuating it was her husband!

Esther looked into Mordecai's eyes. "Oh, Father, it was awful!" She knew Mordecai would never have attended such a spectacle. The unspoken question was why they would want to save such a ruler.

"God teaches we must respect our kings, although we hate the wicked things they do, Hadassah. Perhaps your sharing this information will cause the king to show you an extra kindness or spare you cruelty. Adonai will be your shield and protector."

Esther arrived at the king's dinner early the next evening. When she saw the king seemed satisfied with the arrangement of the room and table set for four, she asked to speak to him alone. He dismissed the servants and turned to her impatiently, "The Egyptian and Ethiopian ambassadors will be here shortly."

Esther bowed slightly. "I'm concerned for your safety, Sire. It's reached my ears that Mordecai the Doorman has heard of a plot to take your life. Teresh and Bigthan are the conspirators. Perhaps others are involved also."

Xerxes glared at her for a moment. She was unsure if he were upset with the message, the conspirators, or her personally. "There are often rumors of assassination, Esther. You know that," the king replied gruffly. "Nevertheless, I'll have Naveed investigate the matter."

If Esther had not been certain of the chamberlains' guilt, she would have felt she had sealed their deaths. Naveed was the cruelest of the king's private bodyguards. Just looking at him made her shudder.

He had appeared one day when she and Della were talking by the qanat. They had suspended their conversation and returned to her tower. As they passed the seven-foot guard, she felt Della shiver in the 90 degree sunshine. *My sentiments exactly*, she'd thought, but a queen could not act afraid of a servant. Naveed would certainly find Teresh and Bigthan guilty of death, and if anyone else were involved, he would discover them too.

⌘⌘

When Esther and Anezka visited the stables two days later, two lifeless forms were hanging from spiked poles in front of the apadana. A sign between the poles threatened a similar death for any who dared to plot against Xerxes.

When Esther told Anezka about her part in their deaths, Anezka sensed her remorse. "Don't feel badly, Esther. If Naveed hadn't hung them, they would have murdered Xerxes. These things happen. I remember several times my father had traitors publicly tortured and killed. The gore discourages other plotters."

"It just strikes me as terribly barbaric for such an advanced people," Esther said.

"You have a tender heart, my friend," Anezka replied, and, seeing the only way to comfort Esther was to change the subject, said, "And it's marvelous the king has rewarded you with a mount. Let's go take a look."

Esther's gloom lifted at her friend's words.

"Which horse have you been given?" Anezka asked as they entered the stable housing over a hundred animals. She inhaled deeply. "I love that horsey smell."

"I sent Acratheus this morning with a message to saddle the horse," Esther answered with a broad smile. "So she should be out in the yard."

As soon as Anezka saw the brown mare, she knew the horse was not for Esther. For once she was speechless.

Esther nodded. "She's for you. I always ride my white palfrey. I wanted this one for you. When the king asked me what reward I'd like, I thought immediately of this little lady. Her name's Stardust. Best of all, she's with foal, and you can keep it too."

"Oh, Esther, I can't believe it! You remembered how much I admired her four years ago. I haven't been riding since I gave birth three months ago, but now I have my own horse and a foal coming! I'm going to name it Danika, morning star, when it arrives, after the horse I rode as a child. Thank you, so much." And she fell on Esther and kissed her, weeping. "I only wish I could do something wonderful for you."

Esther stroked her friend's silky hair, and whispered, "You've already given me the most precious gift of all—your friendship."

# 13

## Isis Vanquished

One day when they were riding on the palace grounds, Anezka remarked on Isis' illness during her pregnancy.

"The physician has prescribed total bed rest, Esther. She may lose the baby."

Although Anezka did not voice her thoughts, Esther was sure she believed Isis was reaping her just desserts.

"It would be a shame for the innocent child to die. The baby's not to blame for its mother. The poor little thing didn't choose its parents."

Anezka shrugged. "With parents like Isis and Xerxes, I can't believe the child will turn out very well. I'm glad I had a daughter. Xerxes won't trouble himself much with a girl."

Esther thought to herself her friend was right, at least until little Aphia was of marriageable age. Then she would be used to form an alliance that would be advantageous for the king. Although Anezka did not refer to Aphia's future usefulness to the king, Esther knew she understood it. After all, hadn't her father used her in the same way? But at least until then, Anezka had a little being to cuddle and love and teach.

How Esther ached to hold a child of her own!

⌘⌘

The news from Isis' apartments continued to be bad. Since Isis had hated her so much, Esther hesitated to visit, but she pondered what she could do.

Perhaps if she made a conciliatory gesture, she and Isis could be on better terms. She finally decided to send an armful of cherry blossoms to the suffering woman. Since Isis was unable to walk in the palace gardens, perhaps the flowers would cheer her.

According to all accounts, she was depressed, dreaded the delivery, and experienced terrible pain in her abdomen. It was even whispered she was afraid. Isis had never seemed afraid of anything or anyone. Even with the king, although she bowed with reverence and dignity, she never evinced the terror everyone else in the palace experienced on a more or less frequent basis. Esther had even seen Haman blanch on a few occasions when he blundered before the king.

The midwives said Sparamizes, Isis' firstborn, had arrived with a minimum of fuss two years before. They had never seen anything like Isis' current condition, and they were terrified of the king's wrath on behalf of his favorite concubine.

Xerxes had even visited her quarters on a few occasions, highly unusual behavior for the king. The court doctor had tried administering various herbs without success. All that could be done was to wait for the birth. The baby was expected to be dead or at least deformed. Whether Isis would survive was the paramount question.

Mayhem broke out in the palace six weeks before Isis' baby was expected. The little one was arriving early. At every court birth, there were several midwives and the court doctor, as well as two of the royal princes to insure a healthy baby was not switched for an unhealthy or dead baby. The princes also ensured the child was not eliminated from competition to the throne just after he had made his appearance into the cold-hearted world. Isis' labor went on for fourteen hours.

To everyone's immense surprise, her baby boy arrived in a seemingly healthy state. He was small, only five pounds and five ounces, but with the royal care he would receive, he should be fine. The mother, on the other hand, continued her labor pains and bleeding. The physician quickly realized another baby must be on its way. In just a couple of hours, another baby was stillborn—a tiny infant girl, terribly deformed.

The palace chose to ignore this second birth and concentrate on the birth of a male who could conceivably become king someday. The midwives and doctors especially encouraged this response in order to safeguard their lives and livelihood with the king. The king named his newest son Artaxerxes.

But Isis was not triumphant at the birth of her second son. She drifted in and out of consciousness, and she mourned for her daughter. Her priest performed the last rites she believed would carry her safely to the next world. And then she electrified the entire palace by requesting a visit from the queen.

"I've never heard her request anything," Parmys commented in amazement when Isis's servant delivered the message.

"She's not going to live long, Queen. I know she hasn't treated you with kindness, but she took heart from the blossoms you sent. Please take pity on her," the servant begged.

⌘⌘

Esther thought Isis still looked beautiful even with the pallor of death on her ebony skin. She had brought a gift of a golden cup for Artaxerxes and sat down quietly beside the deathbed. "This is for your son, Isis."

Isis considered the cup. "You've won," she whispered. "You won the crown, and now you have the king all to yourself."

Esther didn't think this an accurate picture since she shared him with nearly a hundred other women, but she kept this thought to herself. "He loves you, Isis. I'm sorry he can't bring himself to visit you. He doesn't want to see you suffer."

"It's all right. I wouldn't want him to see me like this anyway." Isis paused. "If I could have one wish, my daughter would have survived me too."

Esther gave her a long, compassionate look and spoke quietly. "Losing a child is a terrible thing. Worse, I suppose, than not bearing one in the first place."

Esther's admission of her own sorrow seemed to disarm Isis. The women sat in silence, each lost in her own pain. Esther finally roused herself as the afternoon sun slanted into the room. "You look tired. I'd better be going. I hope you sleep well tonight."

Isis smiled faintly. "Sleeping well's not what I'm worried about. Waking up to a new day is."

Esther blushed at the interpretation Isis had given her words.

"I'm dying, and I know it will be soon...maybe tonight. I have to ask you something."

Esther hesitated. What could Isis possibly wish from her? "What would you like?"

"I have no real friends here, no one to protect my sons from others who will want to ascend the throne. My sons have a real chance to succeed to the throne...provided one of them lives that long."

*What is she asking me?*

Isis was studying her closely. "Will you take them under your wing? Care for them when they're ill? Guide them?"

Esther sat in shock. *She wants me to be their mother after she's gone.* Tears came to her eyes. Children of her own to love!

"You'll probably be a better mother than I ever would have been anyway," Isis said softly. Then she rang a bell and directed the nursemaid who entered to place the week-old baby into Esther's arms.

Esther had not held a newborn since she had been kidnapped from the Jewish community more than five years earlier. Her heart sang, "It is God who arms me with strength and makes my way perfect." He had given her not one son, but two, and by the hand of her enemy!

The expression on Esther's face must have given Isis the answer she desired.

⌘⌘

Relieved of her concern over her sons, Isis fell into a deep sleep that evening. She lay unconscious for three days, then slipped away.

# 14

# Motherhood

Esther felt herself "set upon high places" with her two wonderful sons to care for. She took more responsibility and interest in her adopted children than any of the concubines troubled with their own.

The royal children were raised by servants and tutors. The attentive mothers among them visited with their offspring once a day.

But Esther moved the two boys into a room next to her own quarters and spent long hours tending to tiny Artaxerxes, who thrived on her love. Then she would tuck him in for a nap, commission a servant to watch over him, and take Sparamizes to run in the gardens or look at the horses.

Since the toddler had never seen much of his birth mother, he did not miss her and readily accepted Esther's attention. She referred to herself as Mother, and he soon did too.

In her moments alone at night as she reread her copied scrolls of the Psalms, Esther realized life would never again seem as uncertain as it had in those unsettling days of the contest when she vied with Isis for the crown.

Xerxes, although surprised that she had taken the Egyptian princes under her wing, supported her claims to them. He visited to make sure their quarters were adequate and had been very pleased with Artaxerxes' growth. About a month ago, he had called Esther for a short private talk in the gardens.

"I won't keep you from your duties long. I'm very pleased at how well you care for our children. As you know, one of them may succeed to the throne. I've commanded the scribes to prepare documents to declare them legally your own." He gave her a sideways glance.

"You've done wonders for the little princes, but you've also gained an aura from mothering them. I seem to have chosen a queen who becomes even more lovely as the years pass."

The king smiled in self-satisfaction. "New mothers need time to adjust to their new responsibilities. As such, I relieve you of all your duties, save hostessing at a few special occasions."

Esther remembered the surprising stab of disappointment she had felt at the king's words. One of the chamberlains or guards must have told the king she sang to Artaxerxes during his nightly feedings by the wet nurse.

The king seemed busy with the ten beautiful Indian girls he had been sent. She smiled to recall Memucan's shock at the diaphanous saris the girls wore. They certainly made an exhibition of themselves.

She was sure Haman enjoyed them though. He and the king seemed to appreciate similar pursuits, which was probably the reason Haman was now preferred above the other counselors.

She had not even seen the king for a month. He did not come to check on his sons. Esther wondered if she were already being replaced in his affections.

She shook aside the self-pitying thoughts and reminded herself to pay attention to the little robe she was making Arty. The stitches had become hopelessly crooked when her thoughts strayed.

She looked over at Della, working quietly on a linen robe for Sparamizes. The boy seemed to grow out of his clothes as fast as they could sew them.

"That's lovely work, Della. My stitches are crooked," Esther said with a sigh.

Della smiled a little. "I enjoy this work more than anything else. I just wish I could make my little brother an embroidered robe."

Suddenly, Esther realized the king had shown no interest in Della for four long years, and Della still pined for home. Why shouldn't she go now?

Since Della had put on weight in Persia, no one would recognize the matronly figure as the scared slip of a princess who had departed for Xerxes's court years before.

Of course, Esther and the boys would miss her dreadfully. Della loved the children almost as much as Esther did, but Della would do much better at home. Esther liked to think of her flourishing by the sea. "I don't see why you couldn't."

Della brightened a little, "I suppose I could send it with one of the caravans."

"I think you could do better," said Esther smiling broadly.

"What do you mean?"

"I think it's time for you to go home. And since I'm the queen, I should be able to arrange it. You do want to go home, don't you?"

Della looked a little confused. "Of course, but that's the first time I've heard you invoke your royal prerogative."

"I do it from time to time, when the occasion warrants it, and this occasion definitely does," Esther replied firmly.

Della clapped her hands in glee, dropping her sewing and bursting into tears.

Esther crossed the room to hug her. "Of course we'll miss you. You're my best friend, but I want you to be truly happy. I'll have Otanes find out which caravans are leaving soon for the straits."

Otanes soon reported the departure of a well-protected merchant caravan. Esther was reluctant to send her without any male traveling companions, but one of Otanes' cousins would be a guard so could look out for Della to some extent.

Della tried to calm her fears. "Nothing worth gaining is done without risk, Esther. I'll be fine. You've given me the scroll: 'The Lord is my strength and my shield.' He'll protect me as He wills."

Della had chosen to worship the God of Israel instead of the Greek gods prevalent in her land. Esther knew she was right. Adonai would watch over her.

One day about a week before her departure, Della said thoughtfully, "Esther, where will I go? I can't return to the palace. I know Xerxes doesn't care where I go, but I'd be returning in disgrace. I can't do that to my family."

Esther had been so focused on getting Della home she had not thought about what she would do when she arrived, but Anezka, with her wonderful good sense, immediately saw a solution. "Your sewing's wonderful, Della. If the queen of Persia will write a letter to your mother recommending your services, you can gain entrance without giving away your identity. If your mother thinks it will work to let you stay in the palace and sew, you'll be close to your family. If not, you can always support yourself with your sewing."

Della and Esther agreed Anezka's plan would work. And Esther promised to give Della enough money to set up a shop if necessary.

When Della departed with a letter of introduction and many fine lengths of cloth bestowed by Esther, the queen's apartments seemed empty. Esther had not fully appreciated the many small tasks Della performed for Arty and Sparamizes as well as herself.

Feeling bereft, Esther stood at her windows one evening praying for the safety of her friend. Truly, nothing worth gaining was accomplished without some loss.

⌘⌘

A keening cry broke through Esther's reverie. Odd, it was a Jewish lamentation. What could have happened?

Just then Atossa and Parmys burst into the room, breathless with running.

"Is it Sparamizes? Arty? The king?" To every question, the maids shook their heads.

"Mordecai," Parmys finally said.

"He's wailing," Atossa added.

Esther sank down onto the floor. What could possibly be such a catastrophe? Had some calamity overtaken the Jews in Jerusalem? Or the Jews in Susa? Was Rachel all right? Esther took several steadying breaths.

"He's in sackcloth outside the king's gate," Parmys explained.

"Parmys, as soon as you recover, take him some clothes," Esther commanded the younger of the maids.

But Parmys soon returned with the message that Mordecai refused the clothes. Esther felt desperate. She could not leave the palace enclave to speak with an old Jew dressed in sackcloth. No one knew he was her father. Her servants believed he relayed messages from her to her family. If Esther went to speak with him, she would give away her connection to him and thus her heritage.

At that moment, Otanes and Hatach returned from the gardens with Sparamizes. Hatach was the chamberlain who occasionally delivered a note to Mordecai for her.

"Hatach, quickly, Mordecai is outside the gate in sackcloth and he refuses to change. Find out what's happened."

At the sight of the queen's distress, Otanes hustled Sparamizes into another room. Esther stayed motionless at the window until

Hatach returned with parchment in hand and prostrated himself before her. "My queen, Mordecai sent this document, which proclaims death to all Jews in Adar of this year." Esther took the document and scanned it in disbelief.

"But why? Why would the king do this?"

"Mordecai believes Haman planned this because Mordecai refuses to bow to him."

Esther stared at Hatach. "And he decided to annihilate every Jew in the kingdom because of his hurt pride?"

"Yes, my queen." Hatach swallowed. This would be very delicate. "And Mordecai would like you to plead with the king for the Jewish race." Actually, Mordecai had spoken more forcefully, but a mere citizen could not speak to the queen in such a manner. Who did Mordecai think he was to command the queen of Persia?

But Esther's reaction surprised and disturbed him. With scared green eyes dominating her face, she whispered, "Go back to Mordecai, and remind him what happens to those who approach the king's inner court without invitation. And please tell him, I haven't been in the king's presence for thirty days."

When Hatach returned from his errand, the queen was praying at the windows of her tower, toward Jerusalem. It all made sense to Hatach from Mordecai's reply. In all the time he had delivered messages and waited on the queen, it had never occurred to him— the queen was Jewish.

He cleared his throat and gained her attention. "My queen, Mordecai said you shouldn't think you'll escape Haman's wrath if you keep silent. He said deliverance will come from another source, but you and your father's house will perish. He said you became queen for such a time as this."

Esther doubted she would die along with her people. Only a handful of servants knew her secret, and they would not tell Haman, but she could not stand by and allow that wicked man to annihilate every Jew he could hunt down. Rachel, Ezra, Mordecai, David. Not to mention the blood that would flow once again in the streets of Jerusalem where many Jews had returned to rebuild. No, their blood would not be on her hands.

"Tell Mordecai to gather the Jews in Susa to fast and pray for me for three days. We will do likewise. Then I will go to speak with the king. If I perish, I perish."

⌘⌘

Haman paced around the citrus trees in his walled garden. Why wouldn't that man bow down to him?

The other doormen had been babbling something about an ancient enmity between the Amalekites and Jews. Haman considered himself Persian. He rarely thought of his Amalekite roots. His family had lived in Susa for four generations. Why did his heritage matter to Mordecai?

He needed to get rid of that man. He was like a burr under a saddle, constantly rubbing the wrong way. Every day when Haman left the palace, Mordecai refused to bow.

The king had quickly approved Haman's plan to eradicate all the Jews, but that wouldn't happen for months.

"Parsha, bring a pole from behind the stable," Haman bellowed. He would build a gallows for the Jewish upstart and then figure out some trumped-up charge to persuade the king to execute him. It didn't take much to convince Xerxes to execute a subject. So Haman would build the gallows, think of a plausible accusation, and broach the subject with Xerxes this week.

# 15

# Bearding the Lion

For three days, Esther fasted and prayed toward Jerusalem. No one in her retinue ate except for the princes. She woke on the third morning and still did not know what she should say to the king when, and if, she had the opportunity.

Would he be pleased to see her? Would he extend the golden scepter?

Atossa and Parmys dressed her in newly spun white linen and added the emerald jewelry symbolizing her position. Esther's hands were icy with fear, and she felt ill, but still she prayed. What should she say to the king?

And then, from the recesses of her memory, she heard Sarah's voice singing: *"God is my refuge, God is my strength, a very present help in trouble. God is my refuge, God is my strength, and we shall not be afraid."*

It was a song her grandmother had sung to her on the nights when she had dreamed of her parents burning in the fire that took their lives. She had not heard it for at least a decade, but the music soothed her now, when she most needed it. She still did not know how to speak to the king, but God would help her. After all, it was a miracle she had escaped the fire unscathed. Her life was in Adonai's hands.

Atossa placed the crown on the hair she had arranged so attractively. She added a little rouge to her mistress' pale cheeks. To her relief, natural color was coming back into the queen's skin, and the sparkle was returning to her eyes. Perhaps everything would turn out well for her mistress after all.

After an hour's preparation, the queen looked her best, and a contingent of two maids, two chamberlains, and two bodyguards accompanied the queen to the king's quarters. While one of the king's chamberlains preceded Esther to announce her, she bade all of her retinue to remain outside the king's quarters.

Then they heard Haman's laughter. Esther blanched. If the eunuch had not already announced her, she would have returned later when Haman was not present.

Atossa, sensing her mistress' distress, came to her side. Esther squared her shoulders and took her servant's arm. She whispered, "God is a very present help in trouble," and swept into the room, eyes locked on the king, praying for his mercy.

But the king did nothing—simply sat and watched the queen approach. Overwhelmed by the implications of his stillness and her days of fasting, Esther began to feel dizzy...her vision became blotchy. As the king extended his scepter, she crumpled to the cold marble floor.

Atossa tried to keep the queen from falling, but age and size thwarted her efforts.

Before Esther hit her head, Atossa's burden was lifted. The king had leapt from the dais so quickly he rescued the queen from further harm. As soon as Atossa sensed that he supported all her weight, she retreated to a respectful distance.

"A fan, some water!" the king commanded.

His servants scurried to find the items, and two guards began fanning the couple within moments. The king caressed Esther's face with a damp cloth.

"What's wrong with her, maid? Has she been ill?" he demanded of Atossa.

"She's been fasting, Most High," Atossa replied, "and I believe she was frightened when you didn't extend your scepter right away."

"My scepter?" the king mumbled as he gazed into Esther's face. Initially, he'd forgotten about his scepter. When he saw the queen sweep into the room in all her loveliness, he had been chagrined over his distraction by those Indian girls. Here was a woman, a woman who outshone every other in his empire.

"Oh, my dear," he whispered as Esther slowly opened her beautiful green eyes, "You're my queen. I'm delighted to see you."

He picked up the scepter and tilted it toward her. Esther brushed her fingertips over the top.

Slowly, tremulously, a shy smile began at Esther's lips and crept into her eyes.

The king settled her on a cushion, and a servant brought a variety of drinks. Atossa smoothed her hair and clothing.

After finishing his conversation with Haman to allow Esther time to recover, the king inquired, "What do you request, my queen? It will be given you up to half of my kingdom."

"If it please the king, come with Haman to a feast I will prepare for you tonight." Immediately, Esther knew from the king's expression that she had spoken well.

"Make it so," the king commanded, looking at Haman, who couldn't suppress a pleased smile as he nodded. An intimate dinner party, and the queen had included him!

The king, however, disliked the idea of a party of three. Haman must be dismissed as soon as the meal ended.

⌘⌘

Elated, Esther returned to her quarters, dispatching Hatach to fetch Smerdis, the palace chef. Adonai had been her strength in her hour of need! Surely the king would grant her request.

Smerdis brought fresh bread, dates, and oranges for Esther, who forced herself to eat slowly as she planned a menu with the big-bellied chef. They would begin dining with oxtail soup. Then a choice of white fish with carrots or chicken and rice flavored with saffron. For dessert, there would be honeyed cakes and plenty of fresh fruit.

Esther also remembered the king's fondness for peaches and arranged with Smerdis to come to the kitchens and prepare a peach cake she had often made for her father. Smerdis promised to arrange space for her to work and fresh cream to top the confection. As soon as he returned to the kitchens, he would also send the winemakers with several choice vintages.

That evening Esther, garbed in purple and diamonds, arranged the aromatic roses Parmys had brought in from the gardens. She did not hear the approach of footsteps as she reviewed arrangements for the evening and was startled to turn and find Haman at her elbow. Before she could compose herself, the odious man had grasped her hand and kissed it while murmuring her praises, but quickly released her when they heard the king approaching.

As soon as her guests were settled, and the soup presented, Esther gave an excuse of checking on the children and disappeared. She scrubbed her hands until they felt raw to rid herself of Haman's touch and then swiftly checked on the sleeping little ones.

When she returned, she was relieved to find the king seemed unperturbed at her absence and was discussing music with Haman.

"The queen's melodies on the harp are enchanting. Perhaps she'll favor us with a tune," Haman suggested as the main dishes were served.

The king responded irritably. "She's already done plenty to entertain us tonight on a day when she obviously is not feeling her best. Maybe another time."

Understanding dawned on Esther. The king's thoughts were on the bedroom. Tonight might not be the most opportune time to make her petition.

The meal passed pleasantly with the king lavishly praising the peach cakes Esther told him she had concocted herself, but as soon as the last bites were taken, the king said, "Haman, we have much to discuss tomorrow. Rest peacefully."

Accepting his dismissal without noticeable surprise, Haman offered, "Perhaps the queen wants to present her request."

The king looked at Esther inquiringly.

"If it please Your Majestic Highness, come again to dinner tomorrow, with Haman also, and I will make known my request then," Esther said humbly.

"Excellent," the king responded. "Good night, noble Haman."

Haman quickly said his good-byes and disappeared.

The king gathered Esther in his arms and carried her into her bedchamber while the servants cleared away the feast's remains.

A few hours later Esther awoke at Arty's cries. Gently she disentangled herself from the king, trying not to waken him. But as she pulled on a robe, the king stirred. "Umm, we'll need to do something about that."

"About what?" Esther asked.

"The overmodest robe. It doesn't suit you at all. Those Indian saris— that's what you need. I'll get you a few."

She laughed lightly, "Go back to sleep."

"With all that noise? Not a chance. I'll leave and let you tend to Arty. `Til tomorrow night then."

⌘⌘

The king returned to his chambers, but could not fall back to sleep. Visions of Esther distracted him. She was so perfectly lovely. How had he become so caught up with those skinny girls from the Indus valley?

While he was thinking of the women, he called a chamberlain with instructions for the Indian girls to present a collection of saris to the queen. Then he called for a scribe to read the chronicles of the kingdom. The dry recital should cure his insomnia.

The scribe, woken from a sound sleep, had tried to make himself presentable by slicking down his hair. His tiredness was reflected in his voice as he droned on, beginning with the recent annals of the kingdom.

Xerxes smiled to himself as the promotion of Haman was read. Haman had thrown a magnificent orgy in response. It had lasted a week. Two satraps had drunk themselves to death and had to be replaced.

Then there was the account of Bigthan and Teresh's perfidy and their hanging, due to information provided by a doorman named Mordecai the Jew. If he had not come forward, the chamberlains might have succeeded. They had both served the king since the times of Darius and had full access to the king, his food, and his quarters.

The scribe continued, with an account of a Persian victory over Egyptian forces.

"Wait," Xerxes called. "What reward was bestowed upon Mordecai, who saved the king's life?"

The black-robed scribe searched the page carefully. "None, your majesty. It would have been written here."

The king was appalled no tangible appreciation had been shown Mordecai. He had promoted men to governorships and granted lands for less than saving the king's life. The conundrum of rewarding Mordecai without appearing forgetful kept the king awake for the remainder of the night.

He was still puzzling over the situation when he heard footsteps in the hall and Haman entered for his daily morning briefing with the king. "Haman, my faithful friend, I need your advice on how to honor one I esteem highly for his service to me."

Haman affected a thoughtful air while his mind raced. *The king must want to honor me! What do I want? Gold, spices, women, lands? I already have more wealth than I can enjoy, and advising the king is the most powerful position in the country, so I don't wish to govern anywhere else. And I have too many wives. They aggravate Zeresh with their squabbling. Ahh, I know.*

"Most Magnificent, let this subject be clothed in your robes, seated on your horse, and led through the streets of Susa by one of the nobles who also announces, 'This shall be done for the one the king delights in.' "

The king smiled delightedly. "Excellent, Haman. Perform these duties for Mordecai the Doorman who saved my life by reporting a wicked collusion." He stretched and yawned. "I slept little last night, so will retire. I'll meet you later for the evening meal in the queen's apartments."

Haman left the king's sleeping chambers and paced the dining room. Could he plead illness and delegate his responsibility to Carshish or one of the other princes? Then he would miss the queen's feast. Could he claim Mordecai could not be located? Yes, he would walk to the main palace gate. Perhaps Mordecai would not be on duty.

On his way to the gate, Haman could think of no other plausible excuse for delaying the king's orders. Xerxes became incensed when his orders were not followed quickly and completely. *May Mordecai not be there, gracious Ahura-Mazda.*

But perversely, Mordecai was at his station, and he remained standing as the other guards bowed to Haman. Haman gritted his teeth. Impossible! He would not honor this rebel. But just then

86

Harbonah arrived with a royal purple robe and, after acknowledging Haman, handed the embroidered garment to Mordecai.

"Great news, Mordecai," Harbonah exulted. "The king has commanded me to give you one of his best robes. It's now yours." Mordecai looked at Haman in puzzlement, eyebrows raised.

Haman swallowed and proclaimed in a voice that carried to all in the gate, "The king honors you for exposing Bigthan and Teresh's plot, Mordecai. For your service, you will be honored today by wearing the king's robe and riding his charger through the city streets. I will lead the stallion and announce you. We will depart as soon as you can prepare."

Mordecai, with an ironic smile on his lips, bowed slightly to acknowledge the good news. "Shall I meet you at the stables then?"

Haman nodded curtly and strode away as the other doormen began to congratulate Mordecai.

⌘⌘

Mordecai could scarcely believe the reversal taking place as the haughty Haman led the royal stallion like a common stable hand. True, he did not often announce Mordecai's presence, but Mordecai didn't mind.

Seated up here, Mordecai could spend the day praying for deliverance from Haman's wicked law. He had not heard anything from Esther yet, but this incident must be a good sign. The God of Israel had put it in the king's heart to honor a Jew now, of all times, and Haman had been appointed to do it.

The Jews in the lanes leading to the market stopped to stare at him. Since Haman failed to speak up, Mordecai yelled, "For saving the king's life!" The Jews broke into cheers. Yes, this day must be an omen from the Lord.

Haman slunk back to his luxurious city home, dusty, hot, and foul-tempered. He would soak in a tub of water tonight and plot strategy against the Jews of Susa. Obviously, he would not be able to hang Mordecai soon. He would have to wait until the end of the year when all the Jews would be exterminated, but he could personally deal with Mordecai then.

Haman had just lowered himself into a lukewarm bath when a manservant hurried in to announce the queen's chamberlain had arrived to escort Haman to tonight's banquet. So Haman quickly removed the day's dust from his aching body and scrambled out to dress. In the short time his preparations took, his mood brightened considerably as he basked in the thought of the royal favor he enjoyed.

He set off almost jovially for the queen's quarters.

⌘⌘

Esther was apprehensive. The atmosphere and table seemed perfect, but so much depended on this one night. It really all boiled down to her husband's mood. Was he as pleased with her as he had been the previous night? Or had he slept badly or been bogged down by affairs of state?

She focused on the verse she had found in the Psalms that afternoon. "The king's heart is like channels of water in the hand of the LORD; He turns it wherever He wishes."

*Lord, please save your people.*

As the king was ushered into the dining hall, she approached him with a smile. Sparamizes ran into the room to greet the king and recite a poem his teacher had helped him memorize. Xerxes praised him, and rumpled his hair. Well-pleased, the boy left with his nurse for a bath.

Esther thankfully noted the king's good spirits. Haman entered a bit flustered and late, but although the king frowned at him initially, Haman reported his orders had been completed to the letter. The king replied, "Good, I don't like to feel in anyone's debt."

"Your majesty," Haman replied, "it is good to honor those who please you, but we do, in fact, only fulfill our obligations to you."

This flattery pleased the king immensely, and they sat together to enjoy the feast of camel and fruits in good humor as a harpist and flautist provided soothing music. All too soon for Esther, it was the moment of truth. She dismissed the musicians as the servants cleared the table and refilled the wine goblets of both Haman and her husband.

Then the king fixed his eyes on her. "And what do you request, Queen Esther? It will be given to you up to half of the kingdom."

Esther knelt before her husband's couch. "If I have pleased you, Magnificent One, give me my life at my request, and the lives of my people. We have been sold to be annihilated. If we had just been sold as slaves, I wouldn't even have mentioned it."

Distressed, the king helped her rise. "Who is he who would dare to presume such a thing?" he thundered.

After his difficult day, Haman had drunk too much wine, and his addled brain struggled to understand the queen's words. And then, in the split second before she answered, he knew.

"This wicked Haman," the queen answered quietly, raising her eyes to the king's.

The king flung himself from the couch and dashed his goblet against the wall. He stormed from the room and down to the garden. An electric silence fell in the room behind him.

"Please, please, my queen," Haman begged, "spare my life." He thought of Isis, whom she had forgiven so completely. Surely she could forgive him, but in those clear emerald eyes he saw no mercy.

Esther was thinking of Mordecai, Rachel, Ezra, David, all the Jews in the neighborhood where she had grown up. This madman had wanted to wipe them all out, including the babes. No, she would not ask the king to spare him.

Haman continued to plead, and in his slightly drunken state, threw himself across the foot of Esther's couch, misjudging its length and pinning the Queen's feet. At that inopportune moment, the king, having recovered a modicum of control, re-entered the room, and immediately flew into a rage that brought servants and bodyguards swarming into the room.

"Will he also force the queen in her own chambers?"

Harbonah, who had often borne the brunt of Haman's ill-tempered condescension, quickly said, "He's constructed gallows for Mordecai, who spoke good for the king."

Esther froze in horror.

"Hang Haman on them," the king bellowed.

Naveed covered Haman's face with his robe and dragged him away.

# 16

# Revenge and Reunions

Zeresh had been uneasy since Haman had come home with news of his humiliation in honoring Mordecai the Jew. It seemed a bad sign, so she resolved to await Haman's return from the banquet.

Only two hours had elapsed when Aradai, Zeresh's youngest son, burst into the room with news that Haman was being brought home by the king's guards. Zeresh and three of Haman's sons spilled out of the house just as the trio reached the courtyard. About a dozen of the king's retinue followed, including Tarshish, who was to officially witness the hanging for the king.

Dumbfounded, Haman's household watched as he was led to the gallows. Initially, the boys had believed him to be escorted home in an inebriated state, and wanted to protest the roughness.

Zeresh motioned for her family to stop while she went forward a few steps. "Please, what's happening?"

Naveed answered, "Sentenced to immediate hanging for treason against the queen." They were already positioning her husband above the murderous spike, upon which he'd be dropped and his blood spilled.

"Spare him a last moment with his family," Zeresh begged. But he was already being forced down.

"Avenge me!" he cried before the spike perforated his windpipe.

⌘⌘

Zeresh was stunned. She had never anticipated a disaster of this magnitude. Stifling her grief, she called for a servant to find Parshandatha, who was now head of the house of Haman.

Pressing her long fingers to her temples, she forced herself to think. What was the king planning next? He had executed his most favored advisor. None of them were safe. Most likely the entire house had fallen into disfavor along with Haman. The king was besotted with his queen. How had Haman displeased her?

She would find answers later through her contacts in the palace. Now she must think of safety for the family, and its treasures.

Quickly, she organized the servants into teams to ready horses and carts, pack jewels and gold furniture, and evacuate the fifteen women of the household. It was imperative the women leave at once. The soldiers might return at any time and take advantage of the confusion and humiliation of her family.

Haman's three other wives and dozen daughters were quickly loaded into large carts and spirited away to her brother's enclave. Oibares was on excellent terms with the king's counselors. The family would be safe there for the time.

After the women left, a squadron of soldiers marched through the gate with a proclamation granting the wealth of Haman to the queen. Only a few of their treasured possessions had gone with the women in the three carts. The soldiers refused to allow any of the other carts or horses to leave the courtyard, including the ones bearing Zeresh's dowry of jewels and golden plates and cups. She was incensed, but it was not the time to argue.

Two of the brutes were already leering at her. The leader was more well-mannered, assuring her the queen had commanded no one be harmed and giving her a mount, although the boys had to walk and the servants were detained as part of the booty.

⌘⌘

Oibares posted armed servants at the perimeters of his property that night. The misfortunes befalling his sister's family baffled him.

Zeresh had poured out the story of Haman's last words, confounded as to what had occurred at the king's banquet. Oibares assured her he would find out in the morning and appointed one of his maids as her own, instructing the girl to prepare a soothing tea to help her new mistress sleep.

Then he paced the roof for hours, searching for movement of the king's guards and any further trouble.

He had never particularly favored Xerxes, whom he considered a pleasure seeker. He preferred to find success in his importing business, inherited from his father and grandfather. The company thrived due to the good roads of the Persian empire.

He had never understood his brother-in-law's fascination with the king and all things political. Haman had paid the price, not so much for crossing the king but the queen.

As one of the wealthy elite, Oibares had met the queen. According to his personal observations as well as all he had heard, the queen was very gentle. After all, she was rearing the sons of her erstwhile arch enemy. She took little interest in politics. What had happened?

Oibares called for writing implements and composed a letter to Tarshish, requesting a report of Haman's disgrace. He told the servant to deliver it at dawn so his friend would receive it before he left for the palace. Tarshish owed him some favors. Oibares was confident he would reply as soon as he could.

⌘⌘

Esther had difficulty falling asleep that night. God had not only shielded her, but her people's enemy was dead.

In her horror at the news of the gallows for Mordecai, she had wept so piteously, and the king had entreated her so gently to tell him what was wrong, she told him Mordecai had reared her. The king had been well-pleased with this news and sent guards to fetch Mordecai at once, so she and Mordecai held a joyful reunion.

Then the king had presented Mordecai with the signet ring he reclaimed from Haman, saying he trusted no one as much as one who would save his life as well as rear his lovely queen. Mordecai bowed and pledged his loyalty to the king. Esther bestowed Haman's assets on him.

When the king left, she and Mordecai talked far into the night. Mordecai told her about his extraordinary day, and Esther told him Haman had been hung on his own gallows.

Mordecai returned to his home with an escort of guards after promising to see her tomorrow or the next day, depending on the urgency of the king's business. She had also slipped him into the room where her boys slept. He wanted to meet them in their waking hours as soon as possible.

⌘⌘

The next month flew by as Esther saw her father nearly every day. He had always been disciplined, so although the king's matters took many hours a day, he filled the rest of his waking hours with the family he had missed so much. Since Sarah had died, he had been lonely. Occasionally, he had joined Rachel and Ezra with their three daughters, but their parents were still alive, so their blood relatives claimed most of their time and attention.

Mordecai chuckled to recount the girls' exploits to Esther. Hadassah, named after the queen, was the timid one. The other two had inherited the spunk of their mother and were always climbing to precarious places or hiding in baskets or experimenting with their mother's crockery. Good thing Ezra's family owned a pottery business!

Rebekah was three, and baby Miriam, who learned to walk at nine months, was only a year, and they were already the terrors of the street. Ezra was always deep in study and meditation, and Rachel was left to keep track of her brood as best she could.

Just the other day, Ezra had been in the house while the little ones napped. Rachel took Hadassah to the market to choose cloth for new dresses, but when she returned, Ezra was snoozing in the doorway, and the two urchins had escaped. An hour later Hadassah found them with old Benjamin, a crippled octogenarian who lived on the next street. He said he figured it was better to keep them safely with him than try to send them home. Heaven only knew where they would end up!

Esther shook with laughter followed by tears. If only she could spend an afternoon with her dear friend, but she could not leave the palace without bodyguards. The king had too many enemies. All those soldiers would completely choke the lane where Rachel lived.

Mordecai knew how much Esther missed Rachel, so he arranged to bring Rachel and the girls to the palace with him. Esther was delighted with the surprise, and after posting several chamberlains as well as the nurse and a guard to keep the children out of mischief, the two women settled down for a heart-to-heart, beginning with the day Esther was captured.

When they departed at the end of the day, Esther pressed bread and other foodstuffs on Rachel so she would not be behind in her work and have to rise extra early the next day. Rachel promised to come again when she could get away, but Esther knew it might be months before their next visit.

# 17

# Darkness Returns

The boys came down with high fevers a week after Rachel's visit. Since it was the middle of summer and no one else was ill, the court suspected they had been poisoned.

The doctor, Esther, and the servants spent nearly four days of nonstop care before the fevers were substantially reduced and the doctor pronounced them out of danger. The king appointed two food tasters during their convalescence.

The children slowly recovered their strength and appetites over the course of three weeks. Esther was exhausted at the end of their illness, for she had insisted on staying up far into the night with them. She held and comforted, sang and devised quiet games, and worried whenever she was separated from them. Finally, they regained the energy to play—even baby Arty, for whom the doctor had predicted certain death, though not in the queen's hearing.

So Esther sent them out to the gardens while she indulged in a well-deserved nap.

It seemed she had barely fallen asleep when a commotion in her outer quarters awoke her. Tired and a little angry, Esther rose to reprove the noisemakers, but stopped abruptly. Parmys was clutching Arty while screaming a lament. Otanes was carrying a limp Sparamizes.

⌘⌘

Otanes was utterly devoted to his queen. He had championed her ever since he had escorted her to the palace. Hegai, seeing his devotion to the girl by his frequent inquiries about her, had chosen him to become one of her bodyguards.

When Esther became queen, she had requested Otanes' continued presence. He had seen her at her lowest in the days when she feared Isis and when she prepared her request to the king.

But he had never seen such anguish on her face, as she rushed to him and held out her arms for her son.

⌘⌘

Esther put Sparamizes down gently and bent over him, trying to catch his breath on her cheek, feeling for the beating of his heart. Then she joined Parmys' lament even before the doctor arrived and pronounced Sparamizes dead.

She reached for her other son, assuring herself he was well, and listened dazedly as Otanes explained what had occurred.

"Parmys and I were near the small qanat with the children. No one else was around, although we passed two of the gardeners on our way. Arty had climbed up on the wall and was trying to get a drink, so our attention was taken away from Sparamizes.

"When we looked up and failed to see him, I called out that I was coming to find him. I thought he was hiding. You know the game we sometimes play where he hides and I find him. I spotted his white tunic in the rose bushes right away and sneaked up on him."

Otanes' voice grew even more sorrowful. "But he didn't jump out at me like he usually does. He was sitting very quietly. A pear with a couple of bites taken out of it was by his side. He didn't rouse when I picked him up. That's when I realized the pear's odor was odd. I shook him a bit, and he opened his eyes weakly, but his eyes just rolled back in his head.

"I shouted to Parmys to bring Arty, and we ran all the way back. We met the same gardeners on our way back, and I sent them to fetch the doctor. I'm so sorry, my queen. Someone must have been lurking there, waiting for our backs to be turned, so he could give the young prince the pear."

Otanes paused and ventured a look at the queen. "I've failed in my duty to protect him. I deserve death."

This statement roused Esther. "Nonsense. I should have been with you. Then this never would have happened."

At that moment, the king arrived, followed by Mordecai. "What's happened? Where's my son?" The group parted so he could see his son, still and pale on the floor.

"Poisoned," announced the doctor, gingerly holding the pear up for the newcomers to see.

"How?" the king demanded.

Otanes repeated the story and his culpability. Esther tried to take the blame.

The king looked angry and said roughly to Otanes, "Go look for the assassin. Perhaps he's still hiding on the grounds. I'll deal with you later."

When Otanes departed, Xerxes stared at the boy. Rousing himself, he commanded Mordecai, "Arrange for a state funeral." Without a word to Esther, he turned and left the room.

Mordecai remained to comfort his daughter, but a chamberlain from the king recalled him to his duties several hours later, and Esther was left with Sparamizes as Parmys washed his small body for burial and Arty slept in the next room under a doubled guard.

Esther stumbled through the last rites for her son, leaning heavily on a weeping Atossa. According to Persian custom, her son's body would be guarded outside the city until scavengers picked his bones clean. By then, the stone crypt Xerxes had ordered prepared should be ready for a resting place for his bones.

To Esther, leaving the boy in the open seemed gruesome, but it was the custom of the Persian kings. Little Sparamizes probably would have become king someday if only she had watched over him better. She had failed.

At the three-day sacrifice which the Persians offered, the king didn't acknowledge her presence. The king had not spoken to her since Sparamizes' death. Everyone in the palace knew he had been fasting and was in a foul temper. She wondered if Xerxes was angry with her. She wondered what he would do to her and Otanes.

The next morning was the first time she ventured to take Arty out into the gardens. She would have preferred to keep him inside, but he was getting restless and kept asking for Sparamizes. The cool morning air and rose scents revived her spirits. Arty ran along the pathways with guards in front and behind and Parmys close by.

At a branch in the paths, the high-spirited child chose a way different from the guards. It led to the front gate and the qanat in front of the apadana. The guards obligingly changed direction, and the entire retinue jogged toward the sound of the fountain. Esther trailed along at the rear of the company.

Heart-stopping, horrible screams rent the air. Esther recognized the voice of her small son, who was hidden from her view by orange trees. Heart pounding, she raced ahead, praying that nothing evil would befall her remaining son.

When she burst into the open with the remaining guards, she immediately found him in the midst of a sea of motionless guards. They were all staring at a figure grotesquely impaled on a ten-foot high spike. Parmys tried vainly to calm the little boy who was crying hysterically and pointing to the dead Otanes.

With supreme effort, Esther forced herself not to lose control. She caught Arty into a protective hug, hiding his eyes from the gruesome sight. On the grim walk back to her quarters, the little fellow settled down enough to ask, "Why did they do that to Otanes?"

Esther could not reply. A nearby guard replied gruffly, "Because he didn't protect your brother. The king's making sure that nothing happens to you."

⌘⌘

Mordecai visited Esther that afternoon, knowing she would be distressed by the execution of her faithful guard. He sat silently with her for a long time. "The past cannot be changed, Little Star. It's done, and it's not your fault. The blame lies on the criminal who gave Sparamizes the pear and anyone who knowingly helped him."

"But that wasn't Otanes!" Esther burst out.

"No, I don't think he would have done anything to harm you or the boys. The king's frustrated because the perpetrators haven't been caught, so Otanes became the scapegoat."

"But I told the king I was to blame! Why didn't he kill me instead of Otanes?"

"Esther, executing either of you is not just. You know that. But you also know Otanes would have given his life to protect yours. In a way, he has, and we must honor his memory as one who saved your life. Otanes has fulfilled his role in this life. Now you must fulfill yours.

"Listen, Esther, you've been placed in the king's house at this crucial time. I've discovered that although Haman is dead, his proclamation cannot be revoked. The king has done nothing to alter it, or aid the Jews. Our people are still in danger."

100

"But what can I do? The king hasn't spoken to me since the day Sparamizes died. I fear he's angry with me. Do I need to approach him now?"

"'The king's heart is like channels of water in the hand of the LORD; He turns it wherever He wishes,' " Mordecai quoted. "In a few weeks, Xerxes should be approachable. We'll pray and wait until then."

⌘⌘

Artystone was inconsolable. "He was a good man. Why was he executed, Mother? What will we do? Masa is only twelve. He can't support us. I could do some weaving, but I'm so tired carrying this child." She broke down and wept in her mother's arms. "Otanes is so proud of his three sons, but this time he was sure we would have a daughter."

Her mother made soothing noises. "You're right, lamb. Otanes was one of the best in Susa. He's at the Bridge of Discrimination now, and we both know the truth that ruled his life will lead him to peace."

Atossa paused. The queen had sent her to bring food to Otanes' family, but she would want to hear about this conversation. Atossa was sure the queen would send money to support them and ease Artystone's worries.

Esther had been very fond of Otanes and seemed depressed since his senseless execution. What a king they served!

Not wanting to interrupt, Atossa gave the bread and meat to a boy in the yard and retraced her steps up the humble street past Hammurabi's stele. She joined the crowd flowing toward the king's apadana.

⌘⌘

Parshandatha was very pleased with affairs at the palace. The queen appeared to have no more political power. As heir of the house of Haman, he had assuaged his family's humiliation.

His uncle Oibares had found out about the events of his father's last day of life and passed them on to him. Eventually he would do more harm to Esther and Mordecai, but for now he was satisfied. The queen was reported to love her adopted sons above all else. The eldest was dead. It was well known the queen could not bear any children of her own, so there would be no comfort coming to her from a new baby.

Parsha, as his friends called him, felt confident the murderer would not be apprehended so long after the transgression. The Bactrian who committed the deed had disappeared into the desert two weeks ago, so was practically untraceable. Even if he had been caught, it would have been very difficult to find the mastermind of the operation because Parsha had used four middlemen.

Parsha needed to turn his thoughts to the Jewish problem. His father had shared some of his plans for their speedy eradication, but much more planning needed to be done in order to do a thorough job, especially in Jewish communities as far away as Egypt and Palestine.

# 18

# The Queen's Edict

Meanwhile, the Jewish population of Susa found reason to rejoice. Mordecai, having found himself enriched with Haman's substantial wealth, sold the handsome home and many of the fine possessions and distributed the proceeds to the poor in the Jewish quarter.

The bet 'amma benefited from the windfall, and Rachel found herself in a home big enough for her growing family of girls. Mordecai also employed a full-time servant to do all the heavy work and a pair of sisters to watch over the brood on the third day of the week so Rachel could do her shopping in peace or visit at the palace.

Esther reveled in the more frequent visits even more than Rachel. She was slowly beginning to take pleasure in life again. She especially enjoyed visiting with her well-mannered namesake whenever Rachel brought the five-year-old. Hadassah possessed a natural charm and grace rare in such a young child, and she was already a big help to her mother around the house.

One night when Esther was suffering from insomnia, her thoughts turned to Hadassah, and a marvelous idea came to her. Esther would offer to bring the girl into the palace, educate, and instill fine manners while she learned to wait on the queen. Atossa would soon be too elderly to serve the queen, and Esther would train Hadassah as her replacement. Surely Rachel and Ezra would see the benefits to Hadassah, wouldn't they?

Esther mulled it over all night, and at Rachel's next visit, gently suggested it to her friend. To her shock, Rachel started to cry. Esther put a comforting arm around her, "Rachel, don't cry. I didn't mean to upset you. I won't bring it up again."

But Rachel shook her head, "Oh, no, Esther. It's just what we need. Palace training for Hadassah. I can't do enough for her, and I've just discovered I'm pregnant again. I can't keep up with all my girls, and since Hadassah is so well-behaved, I fear she gets little of my time. I'm always dealing with the other two little scamps."

She wiped her eyes, "I think it's a wonderful plan, but of course I'll need to speak with Ezra. I don't think he'll object, though."

When Rachel left, Esther thought about how different their lives were—Rachel, poor and always pregnant, while Esther was queen of most of the known world and barren. Strange, how life had turned out. But she couldn't dwell on the negative. If Hadassah were to be trained at the palace, her life must first be saved. It was time to speak to the king once again.

This meeting with the king would not be nearly as difficult as the last. Esther no longer feared for her own life. She cared little whether she lived or died, but she yearned for her people's lives, especially young Hadassah's. She would do her best to persuade the king.

If she failed, Mordecai would simply have to change Xerxes' mind. He could use his high position "for such a time as this," as he had told her before the first occasion. Perhaps Esther's work was completed, and God would use another to accomplish His purposes. His ways were past finding out.

Parmys helped her mistress dress in a stunning green robe, and Atossa gathered her black hair around the crown. Esther wore no other jewelry. Her gown wouldn't set off the green of the emeralds, and Esther did not want to provoke the king if he were thinking of replacing her as queen.

She bade Atossa, who had been such a comfort to her on the last occasion, to stay in her apartments. She did not want to raise the king's ire against any more of her faithful servants.

Her mind flitted to the memory of Otanes, and she shuddered, praying the king would be in a cheerful mood today. It would be prudent to send Hatach ahead to gauge the king's frame of mind. So Esther dispatched the eunuch, and paused to play with Arty while she waited.

Arty was a bright little fellow. He and Esther played many games she had devised for them. He always caught on quickly. He seemed to possess his father's mercurial temperament, though, and would fall into a rage if frustrated or bested.

Esther wondered how to curb such a temper, if it were even possible. After all, Arty might become king and take out his moods on hapless subjects.

Hatach interrupted Esther's reveries. "Your Highness, the king seems in a reasonable mood today. The eunuch of his bedchamber indicated he's in neither a good nor bad mood."

Esther nodded. "Today's the day then. I'll be ready in a few moments." The nursemaid and Hatach retreated with Arty between them.

Esther turned to the eastern windows, overlooking the fruit trees and quiet qanat. *Creator God, Maker of earth and sky, Founder of my people, please grant my petition to the king and preserve Your people forever. Amen and Amen.*

Hatach and Parmys accompanied her to the apadana, where the king had settled to deal with the day's business. Esther was comforted by Mordecai's presence at the king's right as she entered the great hall. She hoped she was not sealing their deaths by approaching the king.

She had discussed the situation with Mordecai last week and sent him a brief note last evening. He agreed Haman's declaration must be dealt with promptly, as the king seemed to have forgotten the matter. She wondered if the king would raise his scepter this time or dispense with the formality for his queen.

When she reached a distance of three body lengths from her husband, she prostrated herself. At the touch of the scepter, relief flooded through her, and she begged in a choked voice for the king to put away the mischief determined by Haman upon the Jews.

Tears began to flow freely when she asked, "How can I look on the evil befalling my people? How could I bear to see my kindred eradicated?"

The king removed his signet ring and handed it to Mordecai. "You may write whatever letters you please to counteract Haman's plot. My satraps have reported to me on the affairs of my Jewish subjects. It seems they bring much profit to the empire. The Hebrews of Susa are acclaimed jewelers, merchants, and craftsmen.

"Those who've returned to Jerusalem are rebuilding an important metropolis and reviving the area with commerce and agriculture. I don't know why Haman advised me to murder thousands of such subjects."

The king paused and then declared with a wave of the hand, "He's paid for his poor counsel. Do whatever you must. His decree cannot be expunged because it was sealed with the king's ring, but another edict can be issued to alter the effects of the first. While you're consulting with the scribes, I'll walk and think on other matters."

Esther stood and dried her tears as the king strode from the great hall with Tarshish and Memucan following. Her reception from the king held no warmth, but her objective had been achieved. She turned to Mordecai. "Father, what can we do to stop this slaughter?"

"Not much, Little Star. Men love to fight and hurt others, but we can give the Jews the right to protect themselves and fight back."

And so a new decree was carried by mounted courier to the far reaches of Xerxes' empire. The Jews could band together and withstand their attackers, taking their wealth as booty.

⌘⌘

It had been two long months since Haman's proclamation against the Jews. In the more secluded areas of the empire, the Jews prepared caves and stores for survival and began to disappear slowly from the public's eye.

The remaining Jews claimed they had left on business, relocated to distant cities, or died in unfortunate accidents. Other Hebrews began digging secret passageways under their homes and bet 'ammas, hoping once the events of Adar thirteenth had passed they could gradually and quietly resume their lives.

Many prominent Jews knew they had no way of escape, except for the coming of Messiah. But if Messiah held off his coming, then they would die bravely while doing everything in their power to hide fellow Jews.

When the new ruling, which came to be known as The Queen's Edict, arrived, the Jews danced in the streets. The God of Jacob still watched over his people! Those who were in hiding emerged from their hideouts, and everyone began channeling their energies into securing weapons and planning strategy against their enemies.

⌘⌘

Meanwhile, Esther sadly watched the king depart for the palace of Persepolis, without a word of farewell to her. Mordecai was left in Susa to deal with the king's business.

# 19

# Decisions

Parshandatha was losing ground, and he knew it. His potential allies had fallen under the fear of Mordecai, so there were very few men left to recruit for the cause against the Jews. There were always mercenaries to hire, but as for wealthy, influential individuals...bah, they had all turned into Jew-lovers. His father had a few loyal men in place throughout the empire, but it would be difficult to exterminate the Jews without more help.

Parsha was not certain how he could further harm the queen and chief counselor, but he exulted gleefully when the king moved to Persepolis with a small retinue that did not include his young queen. Perhaps the gods would dispose of her without any more scheming on his part.

His mind returned to his present difficulties. The key to this city was gaining his uncle Oibares' support. His uncle was the most powerful Persian merchant in Susa. Many others would follow his lead without question. But although Parsha had spoken with his uncle on several occasions, impressing upon him the dishonor done to his family, Oibares was not committing himself either way.

Perhaps Zeresh could help persuade him. Of seven original siblings, only Oibares and Zeresh had survived. The younger brothers had perished in battle, except for one who had succumbed to illness. The only other sister had died giving birth to her first son. His uncle seemed to cater to his mother. Parsha would speak with her about the mission.

⌘⌘

On the journey to Persepolis, the king spent a night at a small walled community. After a refreshing night's sleep, the king settled into a private chamber and sent for the chief caretaker of the small but well-guarded hamlet. He smiled to himself when he heard the light step in the hall, but replaced the smile with a glower when the veiled woman entered and bowed.

"May the gods preserve you, Vashti," he greeted her. "How is my son progressing?"

During her reports about studies, astronomy, and physical prowess, the king became distracted by the soulful brown eyes filled with love for their nine-year-old son. The king cut short the reports, pleased to find her beauty still intact after ten years and a pregnancy. She had been only a child when she married him and then disgraced herself. Now she had the figure of a magnificent woman, almost as alluring as Esther's. The king banished the queen's name from his mind.

⌘⌘

His attentions could only be viewed as an attack, Vashti thought hazily as she struggled back to her chambers. He had shown only disgust and displeasure in her since she had disobeyed him nearly a decade ago. What had come over him? What had happened between him and his new queen?

Vashti felt completely humiliated. He had ripped her clothing in so many places she wasn't dressed decently. He had been savage, interested only in satisfying his animal instincts.

*I'll make him pay*, she thought as she crawled onto her cushions, her body screaming with pain. She had already been schooling their son in hatred. Eventually she would add methods of patricide to Darius' education. When the time was right, Darius would strike and avenge his mother's disgrace. She slipped into unconsciousness, dreaming her revenge.

Darius found his mother several hours later as she began stirring. Gleeful at the opportunity to demonstrate the king's viciousness, Vashti described her ordeal with many tears. Darius' reaction was all she had hoped. He raved against his father, cursing him and imploring the gods to banish him to hell. She urged patience and outward submission. His time would come.

⌘⌘

Xerxes had thought he would feel better after indulging himself with the lovely Vashti, but he felt all the more savage.

Thoughts of Esther and her grief over the law he had approved kept running through his mind during the next week. He had left in such a hurry that only his guards, chamberlains, and cooks accompanied him. He should have brought some of the concubines.

Perhaps he should send for the queen. But he was in a foul mood, and for some reason, he had never been able to take out his temper on her.

What he needed was a good orgy! Yes, he would move on to Persepolis, drink for a few days and send for a dozen local wenches. In a week or two, he would feel fine again and be able to get down to the business of touring the city and palace grounds to plan his building projects.

Vashti rejoiced when the king left after only two months. He had visited her several times, and her body bore the marks to prove it, although he had left her alone during his last two visits.

On those visits, he focused his attention on his son, hearing his recitations, watching him sit a horse and practice with his weapons. Although Vashti sensed his pride in the boy, Xerxes treated his son to cruel criticism, holding him to standards for older men.

His harshness only served to fuel Darius' hatred. The young man also believed his father was ashamed of him and therefore kept him hidden away, instead of at one of the palaces in Persepolis or Susa. Vashti knew the king was attempting to protect his heir from assassination, but she didn't try to change her son's perception. It served her purposes far too well.

Esther had thought about little but the king and his cool attitude toward her during the first week of his absence.

Mordecai noticed her preoccupation. "What's troubling you, Hadassah?"

"The king doesn't seem to want me anymore."

Mordecai looked around to ensure privacy for his next words. "Xerxes' moods change constantly, Little Star. We both know this. He favors one and then another. Look at me."

Mordecai gently cupped her face. "You are a jewel he doesn't always appreciate, but fretting about his moods will get you nowhere. You're giving him too much power over your life. Leave him in God's hands: 'The king's heart is like channels of water in the hand of the LORD; He turns it wherever He wishes.' "

"But he could have me, or you, executed."

"Of course he could. We're his subjects, but you are allowing the king to control your thoughts and emotions. You don't have to give him that control over you."

"I suppose not," Esther said with a glimmer of hope. "I'll try to think of other matters."

Throughout the next week, she began feeling much better as she tried to focus on God's protection of her people through the new edict.

She also poured her time into little Arty. She was teaching him to say his letters when she heard arguing outside her tower suite.

She peeked around a casement. Anezka's maid had been stopped by her bodyguards. She could hear her pleading with them, "But it's urgent!"

Esther missed Otanes. He would have allowed either Anezka or her servant access at any time. The new guards stopped everyone except her own maids, Mordecai, and the king. She had to be alert to what occurred outside, so she would not miss any visitors or matters that required her attention. Quickly she sent Atossa to bring the girl in to see her.

"Oh, Your Highness," the maid sobbed, "Anezka's taken a dreadful fall. She's unconscious!"

"A fall? A fall from where?" Esther asked, trying to think why a grown woman would take such a hard spill. Anezka wasn't pregnant. She had never had a dizzy spell as far as Esther knew, even when she was expecting her daughter. Perhaps she had been in the sun too long?

"One of the king's chargers. She coaxed a groom into letting her ride, but the horse threw her, and she hit her head on a stone, and there's such a welt! I've never seen the like. The doctor's with her, but I thought you would want to know. Maybe you have some herbs to help her heal?"

"The herbs I know are mainly for easing achy joints. Go back to your mistress. I'll be there immediately. I should be with her." As she readied herself to leave her apartments, the queen reflected that of course, if the graceful Anezka were to fall, it would be from a horse.

Esther had her friend brought to the queen's quarters and spent a long night at Anezka's side. The doctor believed she would not wake, and truly she slept quietly for over a week. Esther was with her when she opened her eyes a little and moaned. "Oh, my head. Mother, my head hurts!"

"Shhhh, Anezka, lie still. You've taken a terrible fall. I must call the doctor," Esther said. But in the short time it took to fetch the doctor, Anezka fell asleep again.

"She woke and spoke?" the elderly eunuch asked in amazement. "That's more than I hoped for. She's disoriented, which is normal for a patient who's banged her head. The question is whether she'll ever become completely well again. She might lose the use of part of her body or her brain might remain addled. Only time will tell. Whatever you're doing, Your Highness, keep doing it."

"I just sit here and talk with her."

"Well, keep it up. Your therapy seems to be working."

⌘⌘

Artystone had made up her mind. She would become a Jew. Nasha had protested, but not too strongly. She would be more upset when she realized Artystone would no longer leave fruit and flowers as offerings at the tombs of their departed loved ones, but so be it. Artystone was certain the God of Israel was the one true God, and she wanted to worship him.

She had spoken with several of her Jewish customers over the last few months as she grieved for Otanes. They directed her to a man named Ezra, and she had spent time with his wife Rachel too, asking questions she had always wondered, but now finding answers. She had much left to learn. But she knew their god cared about people, about her—Artystone, a lonely widow.

She had worried and worried over how they would pay the man who owned the house they had lived in since she and Otanes were married. On the day the payment became due, she and Nasha had counted their coins again, but they fell far short of the required amount, so no one had gone to pay the landlord. To her amazement, he had not appeared to collect the rent. She had worked even harder at her weaving, staying awake far into the night, shamed that her family must be in debt.

When she finally earned enough to pay him many days later, she humbly took the payment plus a little extra. She knew next month's rent would also be late, but comforted herself with the thought of discharging this debt as she walked to his home early one morning.

But the man said her rent had been paid. No, he could not tell her by whom. His clerk had taken payment and recorded it. He showed her the tablet. The record said the rents had been paid for an entire year!

Artystone could hardly believe it. She still could not imagine who had been able to give her family such generous help, but she did recognize God's hand behind it.

She also believed the God of the Jews would save His people from Haman's edict, and she did not want to have any part in their persecution. She wished to become identified with them and claim the God of Israel as her only deity. So she would become Jewish— today, by refraining from work on the Sabbath.

⌘⌘

Oibares walked in his rose and orange gardens as he mulled over his sister's accusations. He was being pushed into battle once again. He had fought bravely at Marathon when Darius was king, but he did not enjoy fighting. The smells of blood and fear, the sight of gore, and screams of dying men and horses repelled his senses.

He didn't like the rigors of a campaign either, sleeping in tents, experiencing hunger and thirst. He preferred civilized life in his comfortable home with the mental challenge of closing business deals.

But the horrors of battle had arrived on his doorstep. There would be bloodshed in Susa in only six months. The question was which side to fight on. He had delayed committing himself, hoping catastrophe would be averted.

He viewed war as an interruption to commerce. In the end, this conflict would hurt everyone—certainly the poor devils who were killed. The merchants whose property would invariably be destroyed. And anyway, the Jews he knew were excellent business men. They successfully oversaw all types of businesses.

There was a Jewish jeweler a couple of streets from his shop— Old Benjamin they called him. Oibares had been glad he did not specialize in jewels because Benjamin possessed the finest jewels in Susa and the clientele to purchase them. His company stood head and shoulders above any competitors.

But if Old Benjamin were gone, someone could step right into the role of broker. He needed to investigate the terms of the king's proclamations. Weren't the Jews' possessions to be taken as booty by their conquerors? Maybe some good could come out of this after all. And he could appease Zeresh. He did love his sister, and she kept prattling on about her honor.

# 20

# The Balance Tipped

On the second night after the king's arrival back in Susa, Xerxes called for Esther. Esther faced the encounter with trepidation, but the king asked after Artaxerxes' and her well-being and then picked up their relationship as if the last few months had never happened.

When Esther awoke the next morning, she felt confused but thankful. Xerxes rose, ate quickly, and left to meet with his counselors. Esther gazed after him in bewilderment. She never knew what to expect from her husband. She had been preparing herself for the worst, but evidently, he expected everything to return to normal. At least he still cared for her.

A verse flashed into her memory: "Weeping may endure for a night, but joy cometh in the morning." It had taken longer than one night, but apparently joy would return to her life. *Thank you, Adonai.*

⌘⌘

Preparations for the Jews' defense were progressing well in Susa. Mordecai was also receiving reports from around the empire of many choosing to join the Jews' cause. God had made him a powerful figure in the empire, and many of its denizens wished to curry his favor. Not that their support would help them in other matters, Mordecai reflected. He always tried to rule justly and without bias.

However, in this matter they were probably saving their own lives. He was convinced the God of Israel would deliver His chosen with little Jewish blood spilled. Their enemies would suffer a harsh fate. There were already plans in Susa to stamp out the house of Haman by killing every last one of his sons. David was organizing an effective opposition, one swelled every day with the non-Jews who had decided to fight on their behalf. But many in the city were undecided.

⌘⌘

David decided that unless an important figure joined the ranks of Haman's sons, the Jews could prevail, without divine intervention. About one quarter of the city stood for the Jewish cause. Fewer families supported Haman's sons.

Most of the populace wanted to avoid taking sides. They would see which faction was winning, and then perhaps join in, especially for the pillaging.

David smiled wryly and again consulted his map to plan the defense of the Jewish neighborhoods. There was one large area and two smaller ones. The Jews outside those zones would need to move, at least temporarily, though since other families were trying to flee the Jewish hot spots, the Jews should be able to live closer to their fellow worshippers on a permanent basis. He had even heard of an Elamite family and a Jewish family who had *switched* homes.

Oibares had asked Parsha to meet him at his shop after business ended for the day. Parsha was certain his uncle wished to announce his decision on the Jewish question, but which way had he decided? Parsha knew the next hour could well decide the fate of the whole campaign.

Oibares first asked him of his plans to attack the Jews. He pointed out several weaknesses in the warren of streets that would become the Jews' defensive perimeters. "We're in this together, Parshandatha. I've invited about ten other merchants to arrive soon. I think they can become key to our success."

Parsha's wildest dreams were exceeded when the merchants gathered. The stone mason brought his strapping son and his brother-in-law, a wealthy landowner. Artagerses, a jade dealer, and Mithridates, head of the weavers, provided funding and slaves to fight. But the best addition to their cause was Artasyras, owner of a metal shop and many slaves skilled in the art of fashioning weaponry.

Parsha felt a weight he had not even realized he was carrying slip off his shoulders. Their faction had the edge. His father would be avenged, and he would become an important figure in his own right.

⌘⌘

Artasyras watched the young slave hone the sword. The stockpile of weapons had grown steadily since the last full moon. Fifty swords were finished and twice as many spearheads. The weavers would mount the spears on stout poles, but he must show them the proper way at tomorrow night's gathering.

The boy handed his master the sword, and Artasyras ran his calloused hands carefully along the blade. He pointed out one rough

118

spot needing filing and returned to his forge well-pleased. The Grecian boy learned quickly. Soon he would be ready to learn to fashion more detailed weapons.

Artasyras himself preferred the fine work of detailing decorative metal sheets. He was considered an artist and had even carved twelve silver couches for the king's palace. That job had occupied his shop for over six months. It was a pity no one else could afford such work. He had labored painstakingly over the sides of those couches, carving birds, animals, and flowers into the metal. Maybe a few of the rich merchants would order a couch or two for their own homes once the upcoming battle was over.

The swords he was turning out these days were purely functional, no inlaid or carved hilts. The blades were strong and true, but utilitarian. Several in the anti-Jewish group had donated money to pay for the labor. He had donated half of the material so far, and Oibares had financed the other half. They would need more raw material in the next couple of weeks. He would need to see about the funding so he could send a messenger with his order.

⌘⌘

Anezka was recovering her strength. At first she slept almost constantly. Whenever she was awake, Esther or Atossa would spoon broth into her mouth. Sometimes she took only a few spoonfuls.

After several days, she recognized her friend and the servant and called them by the proper names. Her speech was returning slowly, and Esther was pained to think her friend might never recover her characteristic chattiness.

The doctor said she should stay in bed for at least another few days before attempting to walk. She could sit up in bed and feed herself slowly. He still believed she was favored by the gods to have progressed so far.

⌘⌘

Hatach was waiting for Esther one afternoon when Atossa took charge of the invalid. Esther was worn and longed for an afternoon rest but managed a smile for the faithful servant. Although not her personal servant, Hatach had stepped in to serve devotedly when Otanes' execution had left a void. "I know you must be tired, my queen, but I have a scroll that arrived on a caravan from Sipylus."

Although only Anezka and Otanes had been involved with Della's escape from the palace, Esther knew no woman in the harem could disappear without Hatach's notice. He had not commented on her sudden disappearance, but Esther could feel his tacit approval.

"Thank you so much, Hatach," she said, taking the scroll.

The scroll was addressed to the Queen of Persia from the Persian seamstress at the court of Sipylus

Esther rejoiced for her friend, who had written circumspectly in case the letter was read by anyone else.

Della thanked the queen for setting her up as a seamstress. The trip to Sipylus had been uneventful. The Queen of Sipylus had welcomed Della with open arms and been happy to create a post for her at the palace. The royal family had a spirited toddler for whom she often sewed as she had for Sparamizes and Arty.

⌘⌘

With Anezka's health improving, Esther felt she could reschedule a postponed visit with Rachel. The baby was due in about two months, but Rachel was already huge with child, and the friends knew they would not see each other for a while.

Rachel filled Esther in on all the gossip of the Jewish population. When Esther asked about plans to repel the attack, Rachel fell uncharacteristically quiet. At Esther's prodding, she finally admitted

120

Oibares had joined his brother-in-law's cause. "David says his support tipped the balance of power away from the Jews."

"I can't believe God has allowed us to come this far to be defeated," declared Esther. At Rachel's dubious look, she insisted, "The Jews of Moses' day walked away from the most powerful nation of their world without raising a sword. We serve the same God."

Her mind snapped back to Rachel's comment. "David is heavily involved then?"

"Yes, he's doing most of the organizing. He comes to consult with Ezra, but of all the capable men, he has the most time. He never married, you know."

"No, I didn't know," Esther replied quietly. "I haven't had news of him in years. Is he the same as ever?"

"There's not much laughter in the Jewish quarter now, but David lost most of his cheerfulness when you were taken to the palace. "

"I still picture him in the middle of a group, laughing and joking. He used to poke fun at us, straight-faced, don't you remember? I had to be able to see his eyes to be sure he was teasing. They'd always give him away."

"He's become thoughtful these last years. He still plays with the children of course. Hadassah adores him, as do Rebekah and Miriam. He actually gets the little scamps to behave. And he continues to help whoever needs an extra hand or pair of eyes."

"But the David I knew is gone?" Esther asked, with a pained expression.

"Yes, I'm afraid so," Rachel admitted slowly. "We've all changed. Look at me. Even though I'm still a talker, I manage to stay out of trouble."

"How much trouble can you get into while you're that big?" Esther laughed. "You're smart enough to know you can't pull a prank and then run like you used to. You've passed the torch to Rebekah and Miriam," she pointed out with a smile.

Then Esther quickly sobered again. "And I, I've become even more quiet and thoughtful, weighing everyone I meet, to see if he be friend or foe."

"You live a challenging life," Rachel said sympathetically. "Remember when we used to pretend we were queens, with servants to haul our water jugs or washing? Who would think being queen would be like this?"

"I never thought I'd actually become a queen."

"Nor did I, but the Lord had this plan for your life."

⌘⌘

Later that evening as Rachel prayed with Ezra, she asked for God's protection on her friend, and she thanked Him she was not a queen. When Ezra asked about her strange comment, Rachel said she was glad to live in a rented home with a man she loved and piles of washing to do rather than at her ease in a palace where someone evil was always trying to kill her.

"But Haman's cohorts are trying to kill you, matok," Ezra reminded her.

"True. But it's not personal, the way it is with Esther. Haman's riffraff aren't going to succeed in killing us or Esther, but this won't be the last attempt on Esther's life, or Arty's."

Ezra did not wish to upset his wife, but he was positive this was not the Evil One's last attempt to eradicate the Jews. He gave her a reassuring hug. *May the Evil One's next attempt not occur for many years*, he prayed, as he looked at his wife with her huge belly.

# 21

# New Life

Rachel's labor pains began three days later, a full six weeks before her child was due. The midwife sent Ezra and the three girls to his mother's.

After he settled his precocious daughters with their softa and aunts, Ezra hurried home. Clearly, the midwife was worried. None of the other babies had come earlier than a few days, and Hadassah had been a little late. Rachel always accurately calculated their arrivals.

*Could she have been wrong this time?* Ezra hoped so, but he could not quite dismiss the niggling doubt. He broke into a trot.

When he returned, he found all of the Jewish midwives congregated at his house. One of the youngest informed him Elizabeth was examining his wife. "But, but…" Ezra stammered helplessly, knowing Elizabeth, at nearly ninety, had retired from delivering babies before Hadassah was born.

"We felt we needed her expertise," the first midwife told him. "She still advises at difficult births. Here, sit before you faint, and we have to look after you too."

Ezra sank onto a bench, head in his hands, just as Elizabeth shuffled into the room. "It doesn't look good," she told the midwives. "This birth will be beyond my skill. I can brew a potent tea if you'll gather the ingredients, Dinah. Otherwise, you'll have to take turns tending to her. It looks like it will be a long labor. The discharge started yesterday morning, so already it's been twenty-four hours. Before that, she'd been having pains on and off for about two days. We need to pray. Maybe God will see fit to spare either mother or child." Because of her extreme nearsightedness, Elizabeth hobbled out the door without even noticing Ezra.

Four hours later, Ezra was seated outside his door, praying toward Jerusalem, with David and a few neighbors, when Hatach, the queen's chamberlain, arrived. "The queen wished to present your wife with this fresh fruit and bread in order to ease your wife's schedule while she's pregnant."

When Ezra failed to respond, David rose to take the proffered basket. "Rachel's in labor, far too early. The prognosis is grim."

Hatach backed away. "My apologies. I will inform Her Majesty of her friend's plight."

⌘⌘

As Hatach hurried back to the Queen with his ill tidings, his mind raced. Who was Susa's best at delivering babies? Who waited on the king's harem? On Isis? Isis' doctor was fortunate he was not executed after losing the king's favored concubine, Hatach thought wryly, but he wasn't presently serving the palace. Very uncharacteristic of Xerxes to spare his life.

Ah, now he remembered! An older woman assisted at all the difficult births. She was related to one of the bodyguards. If only he could remember precisely who she was, he could dispatch her more quickly to the Queen's beloved friend.

Hatach started to trot. He remembered his own sister, who had passed to the other side during childbirth. The midwife had slashed

124

her belly open to try to save the child. Unfortunately, the boy had died a few hours later.

But back to the harem's midwife. She was a widow, he recollected. Her wages helped support her daughter with whom she lived. The daughter had recently been widowed too. Otanes' mother-in-law! Relieved he had remembered, he changed direction to head to the area where Otanes used to live. The family probably still lived there due to the Queen's largesse. He would go there directly and send the woman to Rachel's aid before he returned to the palace to speak to the Queen. Perhaps the time saved could make a difference.

Hatach had no trouble locating the woman's humble home. One of the boys playing in the neighborhood pointed it out to him. He made his request for the midwife to assist in a birth in the Queen's name.

Since the cottage's interior was dim, he failed to notice the malicious look that passed over Nasha's face when the Queen was mentioned. Of course, she recognized the request as a polite command, not to be ignored, so immediately set about preparing her bundle of birthing tools.

But the look had not been lost on Artystone, who knew her mother blamed the Queen for Otanes' death and her daughter and grandchildren's situation.

Otanes had adored his Queen. Artystone did not, but she had learned so much about her charitable acts and gentle character that Artystone did respect her.

She laid the blame for her husband's violent end at the feet of the one who had ordered it—the king himself. Of course, she could never utter such a sentiment or she would risk orphaning her children. She felt it best to live quietly and try to provide for her children the best way she could.

Her weaving did not bring in nearly enough money, but they lived rent-free, thanks to God and some unknown benefactor, and her mother's wages helped purchase necessities.

"I'll accompany you, Mother," she said. "Let me run the baby over to Elisa's, and I'll be ready."

"But I thought you needed to finish the rug you're weaving for the merchant's wife."

Artystone had just been telling her mother the rug needed finished by tomorrow afternoon at the latest, but she was afraid to let her mother attend this birth alone. Who knew what her mother's festering hatred might cause her to do? She needed her mother, and not just for her wages. "I do, but I need fresh air too. I can finish it tonight."

"When you should be sleeping," her mother muttered.

Hatach, who had been sitting nervously on a stool, rose, and said, "Please, ladies, time could be the essential factor here. Run the child to your neighbor quickly."

"Which way are you going?" Artystone queried. "I'll catch up with you."

"Down the street of the weavers toward the main market place," Hatach replied. "We'll wait for you there if you haven't joined us by then." He took Nasha's bundle and exited the room.

"You don't need to come, Artystone," Nasha tried to dissuade her.

"Yes, Mother, I do."

⌘⌘

Artystone was puzzled when Hatach led them to the humble home of rabbi Ezra. She had been here several times to speak with Rachel about God and his ways. She had assumed they were going to the harem to help one of the Queen's friends.

She started to feel a bit nervous as she noted Ezra among a group of praying men. Why would the royal midwife be called to a Jewish birth? Rachel must be in trouble.

The laboring mother was nearly unconscious when Nasha began her examination. She had lost a great river of blood too, from the looks of things. The two Jewish midwives explained the progression of labor. Dinah, who had gone to gather more clean cloth from neighbors, should return soon.

Nasha felt the girl's fevered forehead and then washed her hands to the elbows. Rachel moaned in pain when the midwife reached up the birth canal into the womb.

A strange look passed over Nasha's face as she felt for the problem. Then her face broke into a smile. "More than one baby. We have too many limbs for just one little one," she said. "It feels like the babies are tangled somehow. Neither is in the proper place for birth, but hopefully I can position one, and the other will follow." After several moments of intense concentration, Nasha eased her arm out, and whispered encouragement to the mother.

As Nasha finished, Dinah returned with fresh cloth and Elizabeth's brew. Nasha sniffed it, and nodded approval as Dinah explained its pain-deadening properties. "The mother needs to keep up her strength. This has already taken too long." Then Nasha continued in a whisper, "I don't think all of them will make it. A happy conclusion would be survival for the mother and one of the babies."

"Poor Rachel." Dinah sighed.

"You encourage the mother since she knows you, and I'll see to the babies."

Two hours later, a beautiful but tiny olive-skinned girl was born. *At least*, Artystone thought, *she will be beautiful when the wrinkles smooth out in a few days.* She cleaned the baby for the midwives, who were still busy with the mother and second child, wrapped her in clean cloth, and carried her outside to her father. "It seems the Lord has answered prayer."

Ezra rose from his prayer mat and gazed at his new daughter, "fearfully and wonderfully made," he whispered. "Thank you, Lord God of my fathers." Then, turning his attention to Artystone, he asked, "May I see Rachel? We need to think of another girl's name."

Artystone's mouth went dry. No one had informed Ezra his wife was bearing twins, and he had failed to guess from the newborn's tiny size. "Your wife will be busy for a while longer. She's having another."

Ezra stared at her, not comprehending. Then a crooked grin spread over his face. "Of course! That's why they're early. My great aunt had twin boys a month ahead of time. They grew into strapping men."

Artystone did not know how to tell this man who had been so good to her that the second child's chances of survival were slim and his wife had lost too much blood already, so she turned away and went back to the birthing room.

She was even more alarmed when she heard Rachel's wavering voice reciting with Dinah's stronger one: "For this God is our God forever and ever: he will be our guide even unto death."

On some visceral level Rachel knew all was not well. Artystone's mother had often told her a pregnant woman knew when the baby's life was endangered or when her own life was nearly spent.
Artystone wondered which it was in this case.

At the very least, the mother should see her healthy daughter, so Artystone brought her the child and watched as Rachel cradled the tiny girl and kissed her downy head with a look of awe. "This is the smallest of any of my children."

Rachel's face became sad, reflecting her worry that the child might not survive, but she appeared to resolutely push the thought aside. "I'll try to feed this one a bit before the pains get bad again." So mother and child rested peacefully as the baby suckled. "Her name is Adin, if Ezra approves," Rachel said in a stronger voice as she handed the sleeping baby to Artystone.

*Adin—slender and delicate*, Artystone thought. *A good name for this baby. She is delicate, but she sucks well, so I think she'll survive.*

The afternoon sun set in a brilliant crimson robe, but Rachel had not delivered the second baby. She was becoming weaker and weaker, and Dinah, who stayed with her except for a two-hour rest in the afternoon, began quoting a shepherd song:

"'The LORD is my Shepherd,
　　I shall not want.
He makes me lie down in green pastures;
　　He leads me beside quiet waters.
He restores my soul;
　　He guides me in the paths of righteousness
　　For His name's sake.
Even though I walk through the valley of the shadow
of death,
　　I fear no evil, for You are with me;
　　Your rod and Your staff, they comfort me.
You prepare a table before me in the presence of my enemies;
　　You have anointed my head with oil;
　　My cup overflows.
Surely goodness and lovingkindness will follow me all the days
of my life,
　　And I will dwell in the house of the LORD forever.' "

Artystone thought it was beautiful. The composer had covered all the times in a person's life—the good ones and the bad ones.

Artystone had always thought about the gods only in times of pain and famine and death. Rachel had taught her God was interested in humans during the joyful times of life as well. Rachel had praised God as she shared the news of this pregnancy. After all, she explained, God created life.

But unfortunately, Artystone reflected, too many times sorrow eclipsed joy when the babe or mother died. Artystone feared two lives would be lost at this delivery, and though Nasha seemed committed to doing what she could, Artystone could not be sure of her intentions.

In any case, she could not tear herself away from Rachel to leave and finish the rug. Nasha and Dinah needed sleep, so Artystone would keep watch.

Artystone gently sponged Rachel's fevered face. The laboring mother dozed between contractions, but the fever was not a good sign. "Artystone, I'm glad you're here," she murmured, squeezing her hand weakly. "Adin...let me see Adin."

Artystone scooped the tiny infant from her basket and placed her on Rachel's chest.

"I can do this again," Rachel whispered. "The pains are getting stronger," she explained, motioning for Artystone to remove the child.

An hour later Artystone woke her mother and Dinah. Rachel had progressed rapidly and needed a pain reliever, so Dinah brewed more tea, and Nasha made a poultice of soothing scents. Artystone suffered with Rachel as she struggled to deliver her second child.

Somehow Rachel willed her exhausted body to deliver a boy, slightly smaller than his sister. Nasha cut the umbilical cord and hastily passed the still child to Artystone. Rachel was bleeding again.

As the two midwives used all their skills to stop the flow, Artystone's attention turned to the child. *Was he alive?* In the wavering candlelight, it was difficult to tell whether he breathed or not. She stuck her finger into his mouth to clear the air passage, and then gently turned him over and tapped his bottom. He did not emit a cry, but Artystone felt his little chest rise slightly. She wrapped him in blankets and held him against herself for added warmth.

This baby was Rachel's first son. Artystone knew the Jews, like the Persians, valued sons above daughters. She should probably introduce the boy to Ezra while he was alive, just in case.

130

Ezra and a few men were still outside praying. "You have a son," Artystone said from the doorway. "He needs to be kept as warm as possible, so come into the house to see him."

Ezra jumped off his mat, and the other men crowded into the house after him. Ezra considered the baby for a moment. "Is he breathing?"

"Just barely. The birth took too long. I'm trying to warm him."

"What of my wife, Rachel?"

"I don't know. She's very strong-willed. She didn't have the physical strength to deliver your son, but she did."

The worry lines on Ezra's brow eased for a moment. "Yes, she has strength of will. But since she can't care for you yet, Little One, I will hold you close." He carefully took his infant son and tucked him under his tunic. "That's good, isn't it? Now I can feel you breathe."

The men crowded around, congratulating the rabbi on his first-born son.

When Ezra began to pace the room in order to rock his son, David said, "Since you are needed here, we will return to our posts and continue praying until dawn."

"Thank you, my friends," Ezra said gravely. "My wife needs you to intercede."

"May I see her?" Ezra asked Artystone when the others had filed silently back to their vigil.

"I don't know. I'll check."

⌘⌘

When Artystone re-entered the room, Dinah was gathering soiled linens and Nasha was bathing Rachel. "Is she ready to see her husband? He's asking for her," Artystone said, looking at Rachel's pale face.

"As soon as I finish here and find a clean tunic, he should come. She needs to hear his voice," Nasha responded.

⌘⌘

The threesome left the room. Ezra entered, still holding his son close to his heart.

In the outer room, Artystone whispered, "Will she make it?"

Nasha answered soberly, "If she lives through the next week, she should. It was unbelievable she delivered a live baby. At least, I assume he was alive. I didn't hear any mourning wails out here."

"He was alive, but barely. Ezra's keeping him warm."

"Good, he has more sense than most fathers. This will be their only son. If Rachel does survive, she shouldn't attempt to bear any more children. Come, our work is finished here. It's almost dawn, and you have a rug to complete."

# 22

# Bitter Victory

Rachel and her son clung precariously to life as the first twelve days of Adar slipped away.

Esther spent the days pacing and praying in the gardens under the watch of a score of palace guards. She wished she could have brought Rachel and the new babies to the palace. She had room in her quarters again since she had finished nursing Anezka, but Rachel had been too weak to be moved.

Then the king had closed the gates to the palace, forbidding entrance to all, and making prisoners of all those inside, including Mordecai. Mordecai wanted to lead the Jews into the battle, but the king pointed out he would be the chief target for the Parsha-Oibares faction and forbade him to leave the palace enclave.

The king also instructed Naveed to triple the regular palace watch to ensure the safety of the prominent Jews within. Esther and Mordecai were forced to watch from the towers and communicate with David through two mounted messengers posted outside the palace walls. Hatach waited in the shadow of the wall with two soldiers while Barnabazus, his fellow messenger, sought the latest news in the city.

A hot and dusty Hatach had returned to this post an hour ago after an absence of two hours with little to report. There were skirmishes at various points around the city and a major engagement just past the main marketplace on the street going down to the Jewish section of Susa. He had circled around to a little-used alley leading to a group of Jewish residences. Several burly Jews guarded a wagon and brush barricade.

When Hatach identified himself as Mordecai's messenger, they sent a boy to the main thoroughfare. He returned with one of David's runners, who informed Hatach there were a few casualties on the Jewish side, but the remaining warriors were holding their own against the Persians, who seemed well-equipped but lacking in leadership. The runner then hurried back to the hot spot.

Hatach was forced to circle back to the palace by a different route since a few would-be Persian soldiers were breaking down the door of a small Jewish jewelry shop on the Persian side of the barricade.

Mordecai was pleased with the news. "They're undisciplined, and Parsha can't control them. That's good for our cause. They'll be distracted by loot or whatever takes their fancy instead of concentrating on the main objective." He instructed Barnabazus to wait an hour and then reconnoiter again.

⌘⌘

When Oibares arrived at the battle, he found ten Persians dead in the road and several injured hiding far behind the front lines.

One veteran soldier with a head wound spoke up when the group was asked for a report. "We charged the barricade like we were told, but there were more dirty Jews than we thought, and they drove us back. The ones with slingshots are responsible for most of our dead. They're slinging broken tile with lethal force.

134

Thanks be to Ahura-Mazda that I bent down over one of the wounded, so the tile grazed my head instead of embedding itself in my chest."

Oibares watched another futile charge on the Jews before riding his mount to Parsha's position. "Tell the men to fall back. We need another plan," he commanded.

Parsha was breathing heavily from the last assault, and his glazed eyes showed no understanding, or even recognition of his uncle.

"Parsha, at least ten men are already dead, and more will die with this direct attack. We need to find another way."

Parsha's eyes cleared and he nodded curtly. "Fall back," he yelled to the contingent across the street. The men began a cautious retreat. A rearguard armed with shields to deflect projectiles covered their escape.

Oibares and Parsha found shade beside a brick home. "This is better defended than we anticipated," Oibares said. "Let's ride to the other streets leading into their quarter and find an easier way in. We can concentrate our forces there, leaving just enough men to fight at the other barricades as diversions. Meet back here in an hour with your intelligence."

"All right. I'll take some men east. I'll appoint ten others to search west of this position."

⌘⌘

David and the Jews hurrahed as the Persians fell back. "Great sharp shooting," he told the men with slings. "You've killed about a dozen of them."

"We won!" a teenager, flushed with triumph, exulted.

David considered him soberly, "No, son. It won't be so easy. Parsha and his brothers are still alive. They're sworn to avenge their father. This won't be over until they're dead. And by the time that happens, Jewish blood will be spilt."

"They've probably gone to assess other ways to breach our defenses," said a sun-roughened farmer, who had brought his family into the city for protection.

"You're right, my friend. What's your name?"

"Jedidiah."

"I'm glad you're here, Jedidiah. Send messengers to our men with instructions to keep careful watch and blow the shofar if the Persians mass in their location. You stay here with these soldiers. I'm going to take fifty men back to the scribe's school. That's a central location, so we can deploy quickly to wherever there's a distress call."

⌘⌘

"We found a weakness in their defensive perimeter," Parsha informed his uncle. "I checked it out. It's not even defended. There's a newly built stone wall on a dead-end residential street. The mortar's not fully dried, so we should be able to pull it down easily."

"Let the men who reconnoitered rest and eat," Oibares answered. "How many should we take to break down the wall?"

"It's a narrow alley, so no more than twenty to pull it down. But we should mass the soldiers, so they can enter the Jewish neighborhood quickly to maximize our surprise. Like I said, it's a quiet street of medium-sized homes with courtyards, so there won't be much resistance at first. The men can secure the street and then turn right at the intersection. It's close to the main barricade. The main force of Jews will be surrounded, and then we can mop up the other pockets of rebels easily."

"It sounds simple. You've planned well, but are there any surprises the Jews could throw at us? Could they have hidden soldiers in the courtyards?" Oibares asked cautiously.

"I left two of the men to watch the Jewish side for any movement. While we breach the wall, they can continue to watch from a nearby tree and report the Jews' reaction, if any."

Parsha replaced the twenty men detailed for wall destruction after an hour of work. Since surprise would be essential, the men had to work slowly and carefully to minimize noise.

⌘⌘

Rachel was trying to feed Joel when Rebekah and Miriam burst through the door. Rebekah was yelling in fright, "Mama, Mama, the new wall's making noise. We were playing hide-and-seek when I thought I heard Miriam behind the wall. I couldn't figure out how she climbed over such a tall wall. Then I realized I was hearing men talking real soft."

Rachel froze. It must be the Persian forces. What should she do? All the men who lived on the street were defending other areas. If only she were well, she could run to warn them, but since the births, it seemed to take all her energy just to move around their home. She had outrun the Persians once. She would have to beat them another way this time.

*Please, Adonai, please*, she begged for wisdom. "Quickly, Bekah, go through the courtyard to Josepha's. Tell her what you heard, and have her send Noah to tell the nearest soldiers."

Noah was only eight, but he would be up to that task, hopefully.

"Hadassah, take Adin in a basket, and go across the street to tell the neighbors to leave quickly because the Persians are coming. Miriam, help me get Joel. I'll warn the neighbors closest to the wall. As soon as you're done with your tasks, children, go directly to softa's house. It's not far. Obey quickly."

Bekah was out the door like a flash. Hadassah left close on her heels, burdened down with her sister. Rachel hoped one of the neighbors would have an extra hand to help her.

She gathered a couple of blankets in a small basket and cradled Joel in their softness, grabbed Miriam's hand and Ezra's scroll of Scripture, and slipped into the street, close to the walls in front of the houses, so the Persians could not spot them.

The young bride from next door would not be home since she had gone to her mother's, so Rachel crept slowly by the first house. She was beginning to feel weak and dizzy.

If she could reach Lesham's family in the next house, they would spread the alarm and help her take the children to safety. Lesham had two little boys and several daughters older than Hadassah.

By the time Rachel called at their door, she felt quite ill, but she managed to deliver her warning. Lesham helped her sit down while she directed her girls to take their brothers and Rachel's children to safety. "You shouldn't be moving around this much, Rachel. Why didn't you send Hadassah?"

"She's across the street, and Bekah went to Josepha's."

"Thank you for making sure we knew. We're the closest family to the wall. Micah moved his family to his father's home last night, so there's no one else to warn, but I'm not sure how we're going to get you out of here," Lesham worried.

Rachel looked at her petite neighbor. "You're not going to be able to. I'll rest a bit and then try to creep back out. Just get the children to safety and when you meet the men coming this way, tell them where I am, in case I can't get moving again."

"I'll hurry to find someone who can carry you." Lesham kissed her on the forehead and bustled away.

Rachel closed her eyes and leaned back against the wall. She wasn't going to give up. She had almost died in childbirth, but she was recovering. "Please, God, be my shield, and make my feet like hind's feet again, so I can escape these Persians."

⌘⌘

"We're through," Parsha told Oibares about two hours after the work had begun.

"Excellent," Oibares answered, "I've divided the force so ten subdue one side of the street and ten the other while the main force marches down the road and to the right, led by the men on horseback. We'll hold twenty in reserve here at the wall and another fifteen or so at the end of the street. I've also sent a messenger to Artasyras to bring his contingent of fighters here for reinforcements. Let's go."

⌘⌘

Rachel had still not moved from her stool when she heard the soldiers march into the street. Lesham and the children had just left. Rachel hoped they had time to reach safety. As for herself, she needed a place to hide. The only furnishing large enough to hide beneath was a long bench pushed against the side of the room. Large baskets and pots partially blocked the view from the door.

Rachel grabbed a few more baskets and lowered herself into the space beneath the bench. Then she arranged two large baskets to completely hide her from view. She hoped the soldiers would not start looting the house.

The soldiers securing the street entered the dwellings two at a time while the others stayed outside the front door. When they entered Lesham's house, the first cursed. "Nobody here, and nothing worth taking. Come on." He kicked over a few stools, and the men stormed out to join their comrades.

Rachel breathed a prayer of thanks. She wondered briefly when she might be able to leave, but she was worn out and soon fell asleep.

⌘⌘

Hadassah had reached the end of the street when Persians began coming through the broken wall. She plucked her sister out of the basket, threw it to the ground, and began to run. Two of the neighborhood children and their grandmother struggled to keep up.

When Hadassah burst into the next street, she met twenty Jewish men and teenage boys. One of the boys stopped blowing a shofar in order to help her.

"I'll be okay, but there are still a few women and children behind me," Hadassah gasped.

As a group, the men broke into a quick trot. She stopped and watched them disappear before she started more slowly for softa's house. She hoped her mother would already be there.

⌘⌘

Hatach whipped his mount as he raced back to the palace. "The Persians broke down a wall and entered the Jewish community!" he yelled to Mordecai.

Mordecai and Esther shared a long, sorrowful look. Much Jewish blood would be spilled today.

Mordecai began to recite a prayer he had taught Esther as a little girl: "'Preserve my life from fear of the enemy. Hide me from the secret counsel of the wicked...'"

Esther joined in at a whisper.

⌘⌘

The Persian troops who breached the wall numbered about one hundred and fifty, but nearly fifty had been left behind to secure the first street. The troops put into reserve by David and augmented by a few more men squarely faced the hundred remaining Persians, led by Parsha.

The Jewish men were outnumbered, but the women and children in the houses flanking the street became aware of the enemy. They climbed to their housetops and began throwing rocks and broken pottery. A few of the boys grabbed their slingshots and aimed at the Persian horses' heads. The horses reared and threw their riders.

One hefty Jewish wife pointed out the Persian leader to her three older children. He was standing not five feet from their front door. "Aim at that one, when I say," she instructed, picking up a large rock. "Okay, now."

Two of the missiles hit their mark, bloodying Parsha's forehead. In that moment of distraction, the Jewish forces surged forward behind David, who impaled Parsha with his spear. With a cry of triumph, the Jews on the roofs redoubled their efforts, knocking down several more Persians, who were trampled.

Although the Jews had the upper hand at the moment, David hoped more men would rally to their position soon. This battle would be won by the side reinforced most quickly. To his immense relief, he saw a Jewish contingent at least the size of his own approaching from the Persians' other side. The Jews surrounded their enemies.

David felt sickened by the sight and smell of human blood. He hoped the children had gone back into their homes before the carnage began in earnest. The sight was grisly even for a grown man.

He set a few of the men to clear the bodies and sent the rest marching back to the bet 'amma. He would join them after he acknowledged the family who had bombarded Parsha. That moment had been the turning point in this battle. He headed toward their home.

As he stood at the door, he heard the Jewish cry of mourning from within the house. Instead of calling a greeting, he pushed open the door. A portly Jewess was comforting a slight woman bending over a basket.

The second woman was doing all the wailing. Eight or nine children milled about the room or clung to the skirts of the women. The youngest two soon began to howl. Finally, an older child pulled on his mother's robes and pointed to David. She hurried over.

"Please, my sister came from the street breached by the Persians. The baby in the basket is dead, the only son of Rabbi Ezra and Rachel. Lesham is frantic, not only because of the babe, who smothered in the rush to get to safety, but because she left Rachel behind. She was too weak, and Lesham too small to support her and take all the children to safety. Can some of your men locate Rachel?"

David flinched. "She may wish she'd died after she gets this news."

"True, but her husband and four daughters need her."

"We'll find her," David promised.

"Did you need something?"

"What?"

"Did you come to the door because you needed something?"

"No, I wanted to thank you. Parsha's death must be credited to your family. You made it possible."

The woman blushed and nodded.

David turned to go and then remembered, "Keep the children away from the street. I don't know when all the bodies will be removed."

⌘⌘

When the Persians at the mouth of the street spied the large Jewish force, they retreated toward the wall. They stayed on the Jewish side of the wall in a force of about thirty. Some of the men had positioned themselves in trees or on rooftops on the other side of the wall. With positions like those, the Persians could pick off many Jews before they were subdued.

David sent one of his younger warriors to update Jedidiah on the battle and their present position. Now he needed to find Rachel before the street erupted into fighting again.

David left half the force where the Persians had been only moments before. He sent a contingent to locate a cart and straw. He took a few men and started toward Lesham's house.

Rachel woke when the door opened and a voice called her name. She lay still, trying to figure out why she was on the floor and why the man's voice was not Ezra's. Then she remembered her predicament.

Surely the Persians would not know her name, but still she waited.

⌘⌘

"Are you here?" David asked in Hebrew.

This time Rachel recognized his voice. "Yes, I'm under here, David." David followed the voice to the bench and swept away several empty baskets to reveal a tired-looking Rachel. Gently he helped her up.

"Have they found a cart?" he asked one of the men who had entered after him.

"They're still looking."

When Rachel wobbled, David made her sit down. When the cart appeared, he swept Rachel into his arms and carried her to the conveyance. "Keep safe," he commanded.

Rachel had to smile when she saw the two sturdy teenagers pulling the cart. "I'm fine. I feel like the Queen." Too late, she realized her poor choice of words, but the boys had already pulled her away from David.

⌘⌘

Oibares knew that if the Jews beat the Persians back from the wall, the conflict would turn in their favor. He watched as David positioned his men and awaited reinforcements. He hoped Artasyras would arrive with his men first. He also sent word to the sharpshooters to aim for David.

His reinforcements did arrive before the Jews. Quickly he massed them behind two sets of men with beams who would charge the wall and enlarge the small breach.

At his signal, the men advanced, but only one side of the wall fell to the beam, so the soldiers were jostled together as they plunged through the wall. If only they were better trained, they would have meshed neatly, he thought wryly, but most worked at occupations other than war. They were banded together by hatred of the Jews, or at least the lure of material advancement if the Jews were defeated.

Oibares thought briefly of Benjamin's lucrative business and his desire to get his hands on it. Since his nephew Parsha was dead, he could claim the authority to divide the spoils of war. The Persians were on the cusp of winning this conflict.

⌘⌘

Esther lay face-down on the floor as Anezka knelt beside her and repeated King David's comforting psalm: "Even though I walk through the valley of the shadow of death, I fear no evil, for You are with me."

Mordecai gazed out the tower window into the city. "We've lost good men, Hadassah, but we've prevailed. Haman's line has been wiped out. All ten of his sons are dead."

"But David and little Joel…"

"Are with God," Mordecai concluded. "I've sent Hatach to the king with today's report. You must ready yourself to speak with him."

"You can do it, Father."

Mordecai tugged at his beard and answered slowly, "No, I don't think so, Little Star. Today was the result of your request to the king. God used you to protect many Jewish lives. The Jews killed about five hundred men in Susa alone, and reports of great victories are still pouring in from the provinces. We won't know the final numbers for weeks, but we do know we've won. Don't let your courage fail you now. You're a Queen, appointed by our God for this time."

After Esther had complied with his advice to ready herself for an audience with the king, Mordecai gave her further instructions. "Haman's sons are dead, but Oibares is still a threat. His support nearly resulted in our defeat. Ask the king to allow the Jewish force in Susa to continue to defend itself tomorrow."

One of the king's chamberlains entered the room. "The most magnificent King Xerxes requests the presence of his beautiful Queen."

Esther stood and smoothed her robes. "I'm ready."

Mordecai gave her an encouraging pat on the shoulder. "You can do this, Hadassah. It's almost over."

⌘⌘

The Queen did not appear happy with the day's events, the king thought as he watched her in his private dining area. She smiled, but the smile failed to reach her beautiful eyes, and she barely touched the delicacies presented to her.

"The Jews have killed five hundred men in Shushan, including Haman's ten sons. What happened in the rest of the satrapies?" he asked.

"The Jews have killed thousands while defending themselves. Of course, couriers are still riding to Susa from the farthest reaches of your empire, so no final count can be given."

"I would have thought this news would please you."

"Some victories come at great cost," Esther responded quietly.

"And what did this cost?"

"The lives of many I've known since childhood, or their loved ones, including my dearest friend's only son. I grieve with her and the other families."

"Do you have a further request, my Queen? It will be given you."

"Those who hate my people are still a strong force in Susa. Please allow the fighting to continue tomorrow in this one city."

"Granted. The Jews can continue to destroy their enemies. We don't want this issue to erupt into war again."

"It won't be the last time. Other nations always seem to target my people," Esther murmured, more to herself than the king.

"Why do you suppose that is?" the king wondered aloud. The Jews inhabited such a small piece of land. They rarely possessed wealth to pillage. Their accomplishments seemed few. They lived as unremarkable citizens of his empire. They seemed to make good tradesmen, but other nationalities also succeeded in business.

"Our Lord God chastises us when we disobey His commands." Esther paused and smiled wryly. "My people seem to live in a perpetual state of disobedience."

"Not a kind deity."

Esther answered thoughtfully. "He is kind and loving, but He is also righteous and holy. He's angered by unrighteousness."

The king thought about a god who possessed a perfect balance of mercy and justice. Such a being was beyond him. He quickly shook the thought away.

"Sire, may I ask for one more thing?"

"Anything."

"Could Haman's sons also be hanged on gallows?"

"Absolutely. Hanging will be a just retribution on a house that stirred up so much trouble."

"Thank you."

"It's nothing but good policy, my queen. But next time you start making requests, could it be more conventional? Jewels, or a banquet in your honor, or slaves?"

This time Esther's smile reached her eyes. "I'll see what I can do, Your Majesty. I hope you and I never see another time such as this."

# Epilogue

The Jews in Susa continued to defend themselves on the next day and killed an additional three hundred Persians. They still celebrate this victory today with the Feast of Purim by sending gifts to each other just as their ancestors did after the battle in the month Adar. This novella is based on the biblical account found in the book of Esther in the Bible.

If you've enjoyed *Such a Time as This,* join Artystone and Rachel's daughters as they travel back to Yehud with Ezra in the sequel

www.ingramcontent.com/pod-product-compliance
Lightning Source LLC
Chambersburg PA
CBHW051834170626
46807CB00003B/1164